SHELTER FOR SHARLA (POLICE AND FIRE: OPERATION ALPHA)

BLUEGRASS BRAVERY BOOK 1

DEANNDRA HALL

Dear Readers,

Welcome to the Police and Fire: Operation Alpha Fan-Fiction world!

If you are new to this amazing world, in a nutshell the author wrote a story using one or more of my characters in it. Sometimes that character has a major role in the story, and other times they are only mentioned briefly. This is perfectly legal and allowable because they are going through Aces Press to publish the story.

This book is entirely the work of the author who wrote it. While I might have assisted with brainstorming and other ideas about which of my characters to use, I didn't have any part in the process or writing or editing the story.

I'm proud and excited that so many authors loved my characters enough that they wanted to write them into their own story. Thank you for supporting them, and me!

READ ON!
Xoxo
Susan Stoker

In memory of J.C.P.
The thin blue line was broken that night,
but a state and a country are grateful
for your faithful service.
You will not be forgotten.

INTRODUCTION

This book is loosely based on an actual crime that took place near Lamasco, Kentucky, on September 13, 2015. At approximately 10:20 that evening, a 31-year-old Kentucky State Trooper assigned to Post 1 out of Mayfield, Kentucky, who was also a U.S. Navy veteran, made a traffic stop on Interstate 24. During that stop, the suspect in the vehicle fled, and the trooper gave chase. When his cruiser drew near again, the suspect's vehicle stopped abruptly, causing the trooper's car to rear-end it. The trooper then exited the cruiser to again attempt to talk to the vehicle's operator. At that time, the individual exited the car and shot the trooper, then fled on foot.

A passer-by saw the trooper on the ground and stopped. His voice was clearly heard on the 911 recording that was released, telling the dispatcher that the officer had been shot and to send help. Also audible was the trooper's own voice, reporting his injuries.

Emergency vehicles could be heard in the background, but they were too late.

Law enforcement from all around the area converged and began the search for the suspect who, oddly enough, continued to post to Facebook during the search. In those posts, he confessed to what he'd done, expressed remorse, and acknowledged that he would never see the light of day. Those posts turned out to be his undoing, as they provided law enforcement a steady signal from his cell phone with which to track him. At 7:00 the next morning, he was located in a brushy area. When officers of the Kentucky State Police Special Response Team converged on him and ordered him to put down his weapon, he instead lifted it, and they fired.

Even more heartbreaking was the trooper's actions. During the first stop, he discovered that the suspect was driving on a suspended license. At the time he began the second stop, he was actively discussing with his dispatch a way to gain lodging for the night for the suspect and the passengers in that vehicle. His attempt at kindness would be the last act he ever performed.

As I type this, I weep. Even with two school shootings having taken place here, the incident that took that young trooper's life forever changed this area and prompted residents from multiple counties to take time to thank their law enforcement officers for putting themselves out there every day. Vehicles all over our area still sport a strip of blue tape all the way across their rear windows in tribute to the "thin blue line" that protects every one of us.

The next time you see an officer, please thank him. Every shift could be his last.

This book is based on the incident described above; however, names, locations, and details have been changed to protect those involved. Any actual information used was gleaned from open and public records, as I have no personal knowledge of the case. I am not a law enforcement professional. I do, however, have the utmost respect for those men and women who protect us, so if any of my procedural details are erroneous, I apologize. This was written purely for entertainment, and I hope it is taken as such.

ACKNOWLEDGMENTS

Thanks to Anne, who encouraged me to make the connection that caused these books to even exist, and to my faithful betas, Tami and Maggie, my proofer, Emmy, and the always-fabulous Drue.

CHAPTER 1

"DAMN IT!" Instead of wiping the water from the windshield, the wiper blades just smeared it until it was even harder to see out. He squinted slightly in the light of dusk and wished he'd washed the glass with his last gas fill-up. *Note to self: Buy a new set of wiper blades*, Carter thought, cursing under his breath because he couldn't write it down while he was driving. With everything on his mind, remembering something that small would be difficult unless it kept raining.

Was his mother okay? Ever since Wilda Fern Melton had fallen, Carter had been on red alert anytime his phone rang. He'd managed to work through her surgery and her hospitalization, then through her rehab, asking the guys to help him out when they could. The smile on his mom's face when Justin had brought her home from rehab in his cruiser made Carter almost laugh out loud. But she was doing better, thank god. She'd asked him dozens of times to fix that banister but he hadn't, and the guilt he felt over her pitching off the side of the stairs was huge. He tried not to beat himself up mentally over it, but it was difficult. *If only* was his daily beratement.

It was hard enough to be sheriff of a small county like Trigg, much less have time for taking care of a parent. *I guess it's a good thing I don't have a wife and kids*, he told himself as he drove. He'd almost gotten there with Mandy, but she just couldn't take the idea of him being out all hours of the night, maybe being shot at, maybe being in a high-speed chase, maybe … So many variables, and none of them good. She also couldn't stomach the idea of holidays without him, and they all would've been without him. He felt it was his duty to let his guys have holidays with their families, so he always worked them.

The thought that he hadn't had anything to eat since breakfast made him want to stop at the next convenience store. If they had some kind of sandwiches, that would have to be okay. Burning plenty of calories in the gym left him able to eat most anything he wanted. Not being in shape wasn't an option. It was bad enough that he was the oldest guy on the force, and that meant the pressure to keep performing at an optimum level was imperative. He couldn't let his guys see him falter.

Henry's Fast Gas was at the next exit off I-24, so Carter decided he'd get off there and grab a bite. He was ready to snap on his blinker when his radio crackled to life, and it wasn't county dispatch.

"KSP post two. Any unit in the vicinity of mile marker eighty-three, shots fired and officer down. Repeat—shots fired and officer down. Please respond."

"Trigg County unit one responding," Carter barked into the radio. The convenience store's exit was eighty-one, just two miles from the scene, and he pressed the older Crown Victoria cruiser until he was moving at well over one hundred miles per hour.

As he approached the area, a chill ran up his spine—there was a Kentucky State Police cruiser there, and no one else, at least not that he could see. Drawing closer, he saw a small, dark car in front of the KSP Dodge Charger, and Carter slid to a stop behind the cruiser. He could see a form on the ground, and he trained the spotlight on his door toward it.

A gray uniform. Bile leaped into his throat as he drew his weapon and opened his car door, crouching behind it. Flashing his tactical light around, he saw no movement, so he crouch-crawled to the trooper on the pavement. Carter assumed he was dead, but the man made a gurgling sound. "Central, this is Trigg unit one. I'm on scene. Need a bus and backup. No perpetrator sighted. Copy?"

"Roger that, unit one. Emergency services are enroute, ETA of two minutes. Status?"

"He's hanging on, but barely. Looks like …" Carter did a quick survey of the trooper's body. "Two GSWs to the abdomen and one to the chest." The trooper made another sound and Carter looked down into his face.

There was no fear in the young man's eyes when Carter said, "You're gonna be okay. Hang in there, bud."

A hand came up and grasped Carter's wrist. "My fiancé … my mom …"

"You'll get to see them in a couple of hours, officer. Help's coming."

"No. I … promise …"

"I promise, I'll tell them you said you love them, but you can tell them yourself." Carter listened—there was no siren sound. Where was that bus? "You're gonna be fine."

"I won't …" The trooper's hand went slack and fell from Carter's wrist, and he didn't even have to check. He knew the man was gone. That was the moment Carter saw movement in the small, dark car.

Drawing his nine-millimeter Glock, he advanced slowly on the vehicle. "Hands where I can see them!" he yelled. "Come out slowly! NOW!" The back door of the car opened and a young woman stepped out, hands in the air, followed by a young man. "Down on the ground! NOW!" He watched as both people fell to their knees, then lay face down on the pavement. "Hands straight out! DO IT!" When they were finally laid out prostrate, he stepped up to them, weapon still pointed at first one and then the other. "Cross your hands behind your backs!" It took him less than a minute to zip-tie their wrists. As soon as they were secured, he went back to the trooper, but he knew there was no point.

Two hours later, it was official: Kentucky State

Trooper Derek Palmer was dead, shot by a woman they were tracking. The two young people, one the shooter's brother and the other her cousin, told them who they were looking for. For seven hours KSP, Caldwell County, Trigg County, and Lyon County deputies tracked her by the signal from her phone in what would be one of the most bizarre turn of events any of the law enforcement members had ever seen—the perpetrator posting on social media every few minutes all night long, admitting she'd done a horrible thing and wouldn't live to see the light of day. At a little after five thirty the next morning they closed in on her, and when she was ordered to surrender, she instead lifted her weapon.

Seven rounds, one each from seven different handguns, ended her life. *Suicide by cop*, they called it. A sad, confused, misguided young woman named Tamara Kent lay dead in a thicket of bushes just yards from a high-dollar resort on the shores of Lake Barkley.

Carter Melton was there. He saw it all. And his gun was the first to fire.

* * *

I KNOW WHAT SHE WANTS, AND I JUST CAN'T. HIS PHONE kept ringing, and he didn't even have to look at it to know it was his mother. She was probably worried sick, but he had too much to do. The first order of business was to turn his service weapon over to the KSP investigators who'd shown up on the scene. There

5

was paperwork to fill out, a statement to give, and a state police psychologist with whom he was expected to meet. Then there was the matter of the two young people who'd been in the car. Since he'd been the first to see them and the one to secure them, he was expected to sit in on their questioning. He wasn't looking forward to *that*.

But it was exactly what he was called to do first. Each of them was in a separate interrogation room. The lead KSP detective, Albert "Bud" Griffin, wanted it that way so officers could compare their stories. "Where do you want me?" Carter asked as he stepped up to the detective.

"Door number one or door number two. Your choice. One gets you a week's time off duty. The other gets you a week's time off duty. Pick a winner, sheriff." Carter reached for the second door—he'd never liked odd numbers.

It opened to a weeping young woman sitting at a table, her straight, blond hair sticking to the sweat on her brow. An officer was already there, talking to her, asking her for her name, address, birthdate, and anything else needed on the customary forms. As soon as he entered the room, she looked up and cried out, "Oh, god, officer, please! I didn't do anything! I'm so sorry! Please let me go, please? I need to call my mom!"

Emotions collided in the seasoned officer. He hated the tears on her face, her pleading, the desperation in her voice, and yet he'd seen a fellow officer bleed out in front of him, his life ebbing away while someone this girl knew played the coward and left him there like a stray dog hit by a car. Those kinds of feelings were hard to rectify. "Miss, please, just cooperate with us and we'll get this over with as quickly as possible."

"But I didn't know she was going to do that! I swear! Please, let me call my mom? Please?"

"How old is she?" Carter asked the officer collecting information from the young woman.

"Nineteen."

"You're of legal age. We're under no obligation to call anyone for you. You get one phone call, and I'd suggest it be an attorney."

"I don't know who our attorney is! I don't know who to call! Please, sir, please? I ..." There was a commotion outside the room and Carter could hear a loud, shrill voice. It was hard to make out what it was saying, but the girl instantly began to scream, "MOM! MOM, I'M HERE! Please, sir, that's my mom! Mom! I'm in here!"

Jumping from his chair and whipping through the doorway, Carter slammed the door behind him and came face to face with a woman who was as distraught as any he'd ever seen. "Is my daughter in there? CHELSEA? Are you in there?" she screamed toward the door.

"Ma'am, you're going to have to calm down," Carter said, holding up both palms.

"I need to see my daughter! Chelsea! I'm here!"

"Ma'am, again, please, calm down. I'm Sheriff Melton. Let's go sit down somewhere, okay?"

"I need to see my daughter! Where's Lionel? Is he here somewhere? I can't get him on the phone! Is Tamara here? I can't reach her either! What's going on?" the woman shrieked.

"Ma'am, let's go sit down. Please. We don't want to have to cuff you, but we will if you don't calm down." He watched as the woman's face contorted and she began to cry. "Come on. Let's sit down and talk, okay?" Taking her upper arm, he steered her down a hallway and into another interrogation room. "Have a seat. Would you like some coffee?"

She could barely speak for sobbing. "I want to see my daughter! Is she okay?"

"Yes, ma'am. She's fine, although she may be in a lot of trouble. We're trying to get down to that now. Coffee?"

"No, thank you. Please, tell me what's going on?"

He waited until she was sitting and took a seat adjacent to hers. "So Chelsea is your daughter?"

"Yes, sir," she sniffled. "She's nineteen. A student at Murray State."

"I see. And who's Lionel?"

"He's my nephew. He's twenty-one, and he goes to school at Murray State too. I thought they were with Tamara. Have you seen her?"

There's no easy way to do this, Carter thought. "Ma'am, if you're talking about Tamara Kent, she's deceased."

"What? Was there an accident? I don't understand!" she cried out.

"She shot a Kentucky State Trooper."

Her sobbing stopped, her eyebrows disappeared into her hairline, and her jaw dropped. "You can't be serious! There must be some mistake!"

"Unfortunately, ma'am, I'm dead serious. She shot a Kentucky State Trooper at point-blank range."

"Will the trooper be okay?"

"He's deceased also, ma'am."

"Oh my god." He could see the terror on her face, the difficulty in accepting what she'd just heard. "Oh my god, why would she do that?"

"That's what we're trying to find out."

"And Chelsea? And Lionel? Are they okay?"

"Physically, yes, ma'am. They are. But we're trying to determine what role, if any, they played in the crime."

"None! I'm sure of it! I just don't understand! Tamara is a gentle young woman. She'd never do anything like that! I can't understand ... Did the trooper threaten her in some way?"

Carter fought a feeling of offense by telling himself that the woman was upset and not thinking clearly. "No, ma'am. Why would you think that?"

"I'm just trying to understand. Nothing makes sense about this—nothing. Oh my god. I just ... Why would she do that? And why is she dead?"

"She pointed her weapon at all of us as we surrounded her and we opened fire."

Her expression changed to one of total disbelief. "No. No, Tamara would never do that. I don't believe

9

you. She wouldn't point a firearm at anybody, not the Tamara I know. Where did she even get a gun? She doesn't have a gun."

"Yes, ma'am. She had a gun, and she used it."

The woman sat quietly, and Carter didn't know what else to say to her. It was a mess, that was sure. Finally, she asked with a sniffle, "Could I *please* see my daughter? Maybe I can find out what happened. I mean, if this is real, if it really happened the way you say it did, I'd like to know what happened too. I'm sure Chelsea had nothing to do with this."

What the hell could it hurt? Carter thought. "Okay. Let's go talk to her." He rose, held the door for the woman, and followed her up the hallway. When they reached the door of the interrogation room, he opened it and swept his arm inward.

"Mom! Oh my god! Mommy!" the girl shrieked and jumped up. In a split second, the woman was embracing the girl, smoothing her hair and hugging her tight.

"Hush, baby. It's all gonna be okay. I promise. Calm down, Chelsea. I'm here now. Let's sit down and talk, okay?"

"Mom, I didn't do anything wrong! I didn't know Tam was going to do that!"

"I know, honey. Come on. Let's talk about it." Carter waited until both women were seated, then nodded to the officer who'd been watching Chelsea. The younger man rose and left the room, closing the door softly behind him, but Carter knew there were at least three officers watching them through the big one-way mirror on the far side of the room.

"Thank you for bringing my mom," Chelsea said to Carter, her tears starting again.

"You're welcome. Chelsea, we just want to know what happened. Can you tell us what happened? Why Tamara did this?"

"We'd been at this rally on campus. It was for gay students, you know."

Carter shot a look at the girl's mother. "Tamara is openly gay," she said in explanation.

"What kind of rally was this?" Carter asked.

"It was all about protecting yourself from hate speech. I'm not gay. Lionel and I were just there to support Tam, you know. She gets picked on all the time."

"I see. So what were they teaching, self-defense and things like that?"

"That's what I thought they'd be talking about, and they did for a while. But then a couple of guys got up there and started talking about arming themselves, about how it was the only way to stay safe. They were flashing guns around, and Lionel and I wanted to leave, but Tam wouldn't. That's when she showed us her gun."

"She had a gun?" her mother gasped.

"Yeah. We asked her where she got it and she said, 'From a guy'. She wouldn't tell us anything else. Then another guy got up and started talking about defending yourself, how people wanted to hurt gay students, and how the police wouldn't protect them. He even talked about how the police wanted to kill them and get rid of them."

That got Carter's attention. "Who was this guy?"

Chelsea shrugged. "I have no idea. I'd never seen him before."

"Was he a student?"

She shrugged again. "I don't know, but if he was, he was an upper classman. He was older than us, or at least he looked older."

"I see." He thought for a minute. "If you saw a picture of this guy, or of the other two guys, would you recognize them?"

"Yeah. At least I think so."

"Okay. We may try to get some pictures for you to look at. So how did Tamara come to shoot Trooper Palmer?"

"Officer Palmer? That was his name? Oh, god. I'm so sorry, officer …"

"Sheriff Melton," Carter corrected.

"Sheriff. I hope he didn't have little kids or anything like that," Chelsea said, tears coursing down her cheeks again.

"I don't know, but regardless, he didn't deserve to die. Do you know why he tried to stop you?" Chelsea shook her head. "Because you had a taillight out."

"Oh, god." The girl looked completely broken, and Carter felt sorry for her. And he believed her too. They'd known there were some radical groups on campus, but this was worse than he'd ever imagined. "But there was something else."

Carter perked up. "Yeah?"

"Yeah. There was a lot of drinking going on at the rally. And when we got into the car, I offered to drive because Tam was kinda tipsy. She told me to get in the back seat, that she was fine to drive. I didn't want to, but she was acting strange. And as we drove along, I could tell there was something wrong. She wasn't talking like herself. She was, like, loud and weird."

That was confusing. "Like she was drunk?"

"No. Something else. I'm not sure what, but something else. Something I don't understand. Oh, and she had money."

"What do you mean, she had money?"

"She had money. Lots of money. Like a roll of bills in her pocket. Lionel asked her where she got it and she said it was none of our business. Answering us that way? That wasn't like her either."

If he was lucky, by the time he left the room somebody else was already checking on this so-called rally and the people involved. He certainly hoped so. "Is there anything else you can tell us?"

"No, but if I think of anything, I'll be sure to tell you. I promise." Chelsea looked to her mother. "Can I please go home now? Please?"

He thought for a minute. "Let me go out and talk to somebody and I'll be right back." Before either of them had a chance to answer him, Carter slipped out the door and found two Kentucky Department of Criminal Investigation agents standing right there. "You guys getting all this?"

"Yeah. Duffy and Atkins are on their way to the university to talk to administration to see what they know about this rally. Oh, and by the way, her story and the boy's story? Perfect match. They're telling the truth. They had nothing to do with this."

Carter checked the guy's badge. Fletcher. "Thanks for letting me know. You guys have a problem with me cutting this girl loose to go with her mother?"

"Nope. And according to the boy, the girl's mother is his aunt and his mother is dead. No father. This aunt, Sharla Barker? She's all the boy's got. I guess he'll be going with them too."

"Gotcha. I'll go in and talk to them, explain that we're going to need them to be available to us when we start sifting through more of this stuff. Did he think he could identify the guys from the rally?"

"Said he thought he could, although I'm not sure. He's pretty torn up. That sister was the last of his family of origin," Fletcher said with a nod. The other agent, Talbert, nodded as well.

"It's somewhere to start. Thanks, guys."

"Thank you, sheriff."

Carter stepped back inside the room and looked from one woman to the other. "Okay. They say you can go, but make sure if you leave town you let us know. As this investigation continues, they'll want to talk to you more, Chelsea, and I have a feeling we'll have photos for you to look at. And, Mrs., um …"

"Ms. It's Ms. Barker."

"Ms. Barker, Mr. Kent is free to go with you too.

Same admonishment. But as of right now, they aren't being charged with anything."

"Thank you, sir. Thank you so much. I'll take them home to Hopkinsville and then maybe they can be back at school by Wednesday," Sharla Barker said, rising to leave. "Chelsea, baby, let's go get Lionel and get you two home. Go on out." Chelsea opened the door and looked back at her mother. "Go on. I'll be right there. Close the door." As soon as it closed, Sharla turned back to Carter. "What about Tamara? I mean, I'll be responsible for ... you know."

"The medical examiner will have the body for several days while the forensic investigation is being conducted, and then it'll be released. We'll get in touch with you and let you know what arrangements you'll need to make to transfer it and do whatever you need to do."

"Thank you. I appreciate it. And I wasn't kidding—this isn't something Tamara would do, sir. Really. I don't understand what happened, but I hope you figure it out, for us and for Trooper Palmer's family."

"Thanks. I'm sure you'll be hearing from us. Take them home and try to get them calmed down." Carter opened the door and waited as the woman stepped out and met her daughter and Lionel at the front door. He hadn't missed the fact that she was a striking woman. He wouldn't mind getting to know her better, but that couldn't happen.

At least not until the investigation was over.

* * *

"Well, whaddya got?"

"Twenty-two-year-old ~~Caucasian~~ female. Brown hair, brown eyes, five feet, five inches, weight one thirty-four. Unremarkable for any childhood trauma or signs of serious disease. Tattoo on right upper arm, strawberry mark on right cheek approximately ten centimeters across. Cause of death, gunshot wound to the chest. Nine millimeter hollow-point glanced off a rib and went straight up into the heart, perforating the left ventricle and the pulmonary artery. Death was instantaneous."

The three men standing over the body on the medical examiner's table let out a collective sigh, and Carter knew what the next question was going to be, so he figured he might as well go ahead and ask it. "And which weapon?"

The examiner dipped his head and looked up at them over the top of his glasses. "Do you really want me to answer that?"

Agent Fletcher nodded. "Yes. We do."

"It came from a nine millimeter Glock, model nineteen, generation four, serial number seven nine seven three …"

"You can stop. It's mine," Carter said with a sigh.

"You know there's a recall on them, right? Bad springs from the supplier," the examiner added.

"No, sir. Did not know that but thank you for telling me." *Fuck it all, guess I'm stuck carrying this damn*

Ruger for a while longer, Carter silently cursed. It was reliable even though it was old, but it was heavy as lead. The Glock was a lot lighter, but he couldn't carry around a gun with a recall, not knowingly anyway.

Carter watched Fletcher shift his stance, his face slack in boredom. "Anything else?"

"I am glad you asked that question," the examiner said, with a sly smile. "I found something very interesting. There were significant levels of three drugs in the subject's toxicology screening. Odd drugs. One was MDVP, a synthetic cathinone."

"Bath salts," Carter mumbled. He knew all about that mess. They'd had several convenience stores in the county that had sold the stuff until somebody caught on.

"Yes. There was also a fair amount of cocaine."

Fletcher's eyebrows shot up. "That *is* odd."

"Oh, it gets odder still. You won't believe what else was in the mix." When none of the officers spoke, the examiner said, "Adderall."

Carter thought he'd misunderstood. "The ADHD drug?"

"Yes. And if that's not odd enough, here's the kicker. Snorted, smoked, injected? Nope." He walked around the corpse and rolled it up slightly off the table until the right shoulder blade was exposed. "Fresh tattoo."

The state police had insisted on a detective from Calloway County, since the university was there, and for the first time, Detective Sam Curry spoke up. "So you're telling us it was tattooed into the skin?"

"No." Reaching to the tray, the examiner picked up a plastic specimen bag. "It was delivered via rapid trans-dermal absorption, placed in the dressing that was put over the tattoo. Between the way the delivery chemicals were made and the open wound of the tattoo, it worked like a charm."

"You mean like Fentanyl patches?" Carter asked, thinking about the drugs his dad had been given by hospice.

The examiner nodded. "Exactly like that."

"So this was no accidental overdose," Agent Fletcher murmured.

"Absolutely not. This was deliberate, and most likely the subject didn't even know it was being administered. And the drugs were chosen carefully. One kicks in fast, another lasts longer, and the third intensifies the first two."

"Wow. So we've got somebody who knows how to take a cocktail of drugs and deliver them through the skin. Can we get a shot of that tattoo?" Fletcher asked.

"Thought you'd want that." The examiner stepped to his desk and came back with a picture of the tattoo printed on a piece of photo paper. "There ya go. That should help. If I were you, I'd be finding out who did that tattoo."

"Thanks. Oh, and based on the findings, when would you say it was administered?" Carter asked.

"Hard to say. I've never seen anything quite like this, so I'm not sure what the absorption rate would be. Not only that, but some people's skin is more absorbent than others, not to mention a fresh tattoo wound for it to enter through. Somebody saw this girl coming and figured it out fast. I guess the biggest question is why."

"Thanks for the information. Email the report to the three of us?" Curry asked.

"Certainly. Let me know if there are any other questions I can answer, gentlemen." With that, the examiner pulled up the sheet and covered the corpse's face again.

As soon as the door closed behind them, Fletcher turned to the other two men. "You know we've got a huge problem on our hands."

Carter nodded. "Yeah. We've got someone out there who's figured out how to dope victims without their knowledge. The potential for abuse here is huge."

Curry nodded in agreement. "Duffy and Atkins are already working with the university. Let me get with them and see if we can track down the tattoo artist who did this ink."

"Sounds good. I'll go brief Griffin and see if he's got some ideas for direction," Fletcher added.

"And I'm going back to talk to those kids. I'm betting they know who did that tattoo." Carter had to believe they did. Not only the who, but the when. And the why.

There had to be a why.

"Hello?" The female voice seemed timid and distant.

"Ms. Barker? It's Sheriff Melton."

"Yes, sheriff. Can I help you?"

"Are you in the middle of something, or can you talk?"

"Can you hold on just a second?" There was a sound he couldn't identify before her voice came through the phone again, at once louder and stronger. "I'm sorry. I'm trying to color my hair and it's hard to talk on the phone with a plastic bag over my head," she said, a nervous giggle following.

"Oh! I'm so sorry. Should I call back later—"

"No, no. It's fine. How can I help you?"

"Ms. Barker, did you know Tamara had a tattoo?"

"No, but I'm not surprised. All the college kids love them."

"So you didn't know she had a new one?"

"No, sir."

"Could we set up a time for me to talk to your daughter and your nephew?"

"Certainly. I mean, can't it wait, though? We're going to have a funeral to do and—"

"No, ma'am. It can't." Carter knew she was going to start asking questions, and he really didn't want to have to answer them. "There's a bit of urgency in this request."

"I see. Well, they're at the school now, but they'll both be coming home tomorrow and staying the weekend." The phone was silent for a few seconds and then she asked, "Have you found out anything about Tamara? I mean, her death? Why she was acting that way and why she did the stuff she did?"

"Actually, yes, but I'd rather not get into that on the phone." Not only did he not want to talk about it on the phone, he didn't want her to be able to tell Chelsea and Lionel what had been found before he got the chance. If they did actually have something to do with it, that would give them time to tip off the person or people involved. He couldn't risk that.

"Okay. So maybe tomorrow evening after seven?"

"I'll be there. Thank you, Ms. Barker."

"You're welcome, sheriff. Goodbye."

Carter sat there for a few seconds, thinking about the tattoo, but then his thoughts shifted to the woman he'd just spoken with. He had no reason to think she had anything to do with any of the goings-on, but he hoped when he gave her the information he'd received, she'd make sure Chelsea and Lionel cooperated.

It was almost five before he headed back to the Trigg County Sheriff's Department's office. "Anything going on that I should know about?" Carter asked his chief deputy, Gray Lewis, through the cracked office door as he changed into street clothes.

"Nope. Arrested Ben Taylor again."

"Another DUI?"

"Yep. Ten thirty in the morning at that. They guy just can't seem to help himself," Gray said with a grin.

But Carter was in no mood for witty banter as he zipped his jeans and buckled his belt. "No. He can't. Anything else?"

"Judge Michaels threw out four of our ten traffic citations."

Strolling out into the main office, Carter looked from the stack of papers on the front desk and back to Gray with one jacked-up one eyebrow. "And why was that?"

"Said the ticket wasn't filled out properly."

"Don't tell me—Edwards."

"Yep."

The sheriff shook his head. That young deputy wasn't going to make it if he didn't get his shit together. "I'll have a talk with him. Anything else?"

There was a glint of mischief in Gray's eyes. "Yeah. Penny came by here again today looking for you."

"Well, fuck me," Carter mumbled under his breath.

That set Gray laughing. "She wants to!"

"Well, she can want in one hand and shit in the other and see which one fills up fastest. She's barking up the wrong tree here," Carter announced to no one in particular.

"Oh, come on, Carter! She's a good-looking woman."

"Yeah, and I'm up for reelection next year. Want to fuck *that* up?"

Gray shook his head. "Nope. I like working for you."

"Good. Then discourage her every chance you get." God, it had been a long day and he was tired. He sure didn't need the local Methodist minister's ex-wife sniffing around. Before he could say another word, his phone rang. "Yeah, Mom?"

"Carter! Are you busy?"

Am I busy? I'm always *busy*, he wanted to say, but instead he simply said, "No. What's up?"

"My car won't start. Could you come over and take a look at it?"

"Sure. Be there in a few minutes."

"Thank you, son."

"You're welcome, Mom. See you in a few." As soon as he punched END on the screen, he turned to Gray. "I've got to go. Tell the guys I'll check on them before I go to bed."

"Will do, sheriff. Have a pleasant evening," Gray answered.

"Yeah, yeah. Right. Pleasant evening," Carter was muttering as he stepped out the door. Would it never end?

Two hours. It took two hours for him to figure out what was wrong with his mother's car. "I can't fix this, Mom. You'll have to call a tow truck and let the mechanic fix it," he informed her as he stepped into the house.

"Rocky's?"

"Yeah. I trust him."

"Okay. Want something to eat?" Her tone almost apologetic, and he hoped he hadn't made her feel bad for calling him. That wasn't his intention at all.

"No, thanks. I'm gonna go. Got some paperwork to do." *Liar. You're gonna go have a drink*, he told himself.

"Okay. Well, thanks again, son. I love you," Wilda Fern told him and patted his cheek.

He leaned down and kissed hers. "I love you too, Mom. Talk to you tomorrow."

"Okay. Night." When he slipped behind the Crown Victoria's steering wheel, he could still see her standing there in the doorway, watching him leave. He knew she was lonely. He was lonely too.

Just as he pulled out of her driveway, something occurred to him. There was a bar he'd been wanting to explore in Hopkinsville, The Fat Rabbit. He'd heard they had a great jalapeno and Monterey Jack burger, and what better place to ask about a tattoo than a bar? Rolling toward I-24, he pulled onto the interstate and let the big car cruise along. He was pretty sure a burger and a beer wouldn't erase the horrible day he'd had.

But it certainly couldn't hurt.

CHAPTER 2

IT ONLY TOOK about twenty-five minutes to get there, and he smiled when he took in the bar's façade. The ancient brick building had huge plate glass windows, and through them he could see old-fashioned tavern-style lighting, its amber bulbs casting a golden glow even on the sidewalk. The evening was warm, and the front door stood open, allowing voices to spill out into the air on the street.

There was no sign inside the doorway asking patrons to wait to be seated, so he strolled to the bar and took a stool. The bartender turned and smiled. "Hey there! What'll it be?"

"Whaddya have on tap?" After listening to the recitation of domestics and imports, Carter settled on a Stella Artois. "I hear you have a great burger or two," he said before the barkeep could walk away.

"Sure do. I think our jalapeno and Monterey Jack is the best."

"I've heard that too. Could I have one with pub chips?"

"Coming right up," the younger man said with a smile as he walked away. In seconds, a frosty mug of amber-colored liquid appeared in front of Carter and he took a long, deep draw from it. God, that was exactly what he needed!

As he sat, he turned slightly to look around. It was the usual kind of crowd in a bar like that—"like that" being decidedly *not* hip. The old school vibe was alive and well within its aging walls. There were a few couples, some with other couples and others who looked like they were having a simple date night. Against the far wall sat a table with a checker board on it, and two guys bent over it playing, one about his age and one much younger. Father and son maybe? When he turned the other way to check out that end of the building, he almost choked.

Sharla Barker was sitting at the other end of the bar. And she was alone.

Awww, hell. This is not *how I'd pictured this evening going*, he told himself. Which would be worse? Going down there and speaking to her? Or waiting to see if she recognized him and came his direction? Carter rolled his eyes and sighed. *Might as well get it over with*. He stepped up quietly, beer in his hand, and asked, "Mind if I sit?"

She spun to face him and her eyes went wide. "Sheriff! No, please. Have a seat. What are you doing here?"

"I've been wanting to check this place out. I hear the food's good."

"It is. I come here every Thursday night. It's ladies' night and it's the only time I can afford to take myself out to eat," she answered, her cheeks pinking. Carter thought that was unbelievably cute—and a bit sad too.

"You won't have to worry about that tonight. It's on me," he said and took another sip of his beer. *Holy fuck, this is a bad idea*, he thought, chastising himself. *Oh, well, it's done now.*

The woman's face reddened. "That's not necessary."

"I insist. You've had a shitty week. It's the least I can do."

He thought he saw a tear in the corner of her eye before she said, "Well, thank you. That's very nice of you."

"You're welcome."

"So you said you had some news about Tamara?"

Well, shit, here goes the evening, he groused internally. "Actually, yeah, I do. Her cause of death was a gunshot wound." *Should I?* he wondered. *What the hell.* "From my weapon."

She was silent for a few seconds, then said, "Well, thank you for being honest."

"Feel like I have to be. Even though there were several wounds, that was the deciding one. But we're trying to unravel a bit of a puzzle." Deciding not to hesitate, he whipped out the picture of the tattoo. "Ever seen this before?"

27

Sharla took it in her hands and held it up to the light. "Not that I recall. What is it?"

"That's the tattoo."

She shook her head, still staring at it. "No. I've never seen anything like it. What is that design?"

"We don't know, but I have to believe it has some meaning. No idea at all?" The woman shook her head. *Should I tell her about the drugs?* In that moment, he decided not to. He'd tell all three of them the next evening when he went to talk to the kids. Until then, he'd keep that to himself. "And you're Lionel's aunt?"

She nodded, her face sad. "Yes. My sister's kids. Their dad was killed in a robbery gone wrong, and my sister died of cancer four years ago. It's been left up to me to take care of them."

"And Chelsea's your only daughter?"

That got another nod. "Yes. Her father and I divorced when she was eight. We haven't seen him since." He had to admit, the woman had it rough. Three kids, two of whom weren't even hers, and she was going it alone. His hat was definitely off to her.

Throw her a scrap, Melton. The woman needs encouragement. "Chelsea seems like a good kid."

"She is. Honor roll student, dean's list, works almost full time."

"Wow. That's something. So does she live on campus?"

He watched as Sharla's hands slid up and down her beer bottle, and he wondered what they'd feel like gripping something of his that would be just as hard but a lot warmer. "Yeah. The three of them lived in family housing. That's supposed to be reserved for families with children, but their advisors all got together and found a way for it to happen since they really couldn't afford dorm fees. They're all going to school on student loans. I can barely make ends meet as it is. I can't pay for college for one kid, much less three. Ridiculously expensive."

"It was ridiculous when I was in college. I can't imagine what it costs now."

"You went to college?" Carter nodded. "What was your major? Oh, wait. Let me guess. Criminal justice."

"Yes, ma'am. Sure was. Master's degree."

"And how long have you been sheriff?"

"Going on fourteen years now," Carter answered, then realized how pathetic that sounded. Sheriff of a tiny county in western Kentucky. It was certainly no claim to fame.

"Wow! That's quite a career! I'm assuming you worked for them as a deputy before you became sheriff."

"Yes, ma'am. Deputy, then detective, then ran for sheriff and won. And I've won the last three elections, so I guess they like me well enough." He took a draw of his beer and thought about how many sleepless nights he'd spent on the job.

"You're very professional. I think I'd be comfortable with you as sheriff if I lived in your county." The woman smiled as she said it, and Carter almost blushed. Kindness like that wasn't something he ran into every day. Most days he spent his time with people who'd rather kill him than look at him.

"Thank you. That's a really nice thing to say."

"You're a nice man." She turned back to her beer bottle and Carter couldn't help but notice the slope of her cheeks. He'd seen prettier women, but she was … striking. That was the term he'd use. Almost regal.

Small talk wasn't his thing, so it took him a minute to fish around for something to say. "So where do you work?"

"The hospital."

"Methodist or County?"

"County. I'm a respiratory therapist. I work mostly with postoperative patients. You know, trying to get the anesthesia out of their lungs and get their breathing back to normal."

"Sounds like an interesting job." Actually, it didn't, but he didn't know what else to say.

"It's okay, I guess. I wanted to go into radiology. I find all the equipment and technology fascinating. But that just wasn't in the cards. The courses were full, and they were begging for respiratory people, so I just signed on and here I am."

"Here you go, ma'am," the bartender said as he appeared with Ms. Barker's food. "Do you need some ranch dressing for dipping?"

"Yes, please," she answered, then turned to Carter. "They have the absolute best chicken tenders on the planet. I love them. What did you order?"

"One of those burgers. Oh, here it comes." The

bartender stepped up and placed the plate in front of Carter. "That looks delicious."

"Thank you, sir! Need ketchup to go with those fries?"

"Yes, please." He watched as discreetly as possible as Ms. Barker dipped one of the chicken tenders and chewed slowly, almost meditatively, and he wondered if that was her way of enjoying the one meal she bought for herself every week. The bartender returned with his ketchup and the two of them ate in silence.

He was halfway through his burger before she spoke. "So what's going to happen to Chelsea and Lionel?"

"Nothing, as far as I know, although we sure would like to have their help."

"Oh, you'll get that." Dabbing at the corners of her mouth with her napkin, she smiled. "They'll cooperate or I'll have their hide. I'm just glad my sister's not around for me to have to tell her how I screwed up with her kids."

"You didn't screw up. Your niece was twenty-two. An adult. You couldn't control that."

Her eyes were sad, a thing that tore at his heart, knowing how hard she worked and the difficulties she had to be facing. "If I'd spent more time with them, maybe she—"

"That's nonsense. They were college kids. They don't want to spend time with parents, or aunts, or anybody who's an adult or represents authority of any kind. You know that."

"I guess, but still—"

"Stop beating yourself up. You've done a good job with Chelsea, and Lionel seems like a good kid."

Ms. Barker let out a deep sigh. "It's just so hard." As soon as the phrase slipped from her tongue, Carter had an overwhelming urge to take her hand and just hold it. She needed consolation. Validation. Encouragement. Peace. And an idea struck him.

"Finish your food and let's go take a walk, whaddya say? It's a pretty night." A smile split her face and Carter felt like some kind of genius. He'd made her smile! Considering what was going on with her, that was huge.

"You know, that sounds nice. You're on!" she said and tucked into her food. There was a cheerfulness to her voice that hadn't been there before, and his heart fluttered for a few seconds. Why did making her feel better make *him* feel better?

Fifteen minutes and one brief half-hearted argument later, Carter paid the entire tab and turned to smile at her. "Ready for that walk?"

"Sure!" He watched her stroll toward the door and noticed the beautiful slope of her ass, its perfect heart shape swaying gently, and something below his belt clenched. God, that was a fine ass! *Stop it, Melton!* he chided himself, but there was no denying it. She was a good-looking woman, not to mention intelligent and conscientious, all qualities he valued highly. Nothing she'd said seemed dishonest either, and that was at the top of his list. "Want to walk over toward the courthouse? The fountain is pretty in the evenings," she asked, and there was a gentleness in her voice that he hadn't heard earlier.

"Sounds great." Carter shoved both hands into his pockets and wandered along beside her. From time to time she'd point at something and tell him about it, this building or that cornerstone, or a particular tree or sign. It was obvious she'd lived there all her life and she was proud of her hometown. They were almost to the courthouse when he said, "Last time I was here, I was delivering a prisoner to Western State."

To his surprise, he saw her shudder before she said, "Yeah. We have a family history with that hospital."

"Oh?"

"Yeah. My grandmother died there."

"A patient?"

"No. A nurse. Killed by a patient. Schizophrenic. Have you ever been inside? I mean, really inside?" she asked, her pace slowing.

"Not really."

"Well, then, you just can't know. I had to do a two-week practicum there. Oh my god, it was terrifying. Chilling. I swore then that I'd never go back, and I haven't. You couldn't pay me enough to work there."

"I'm so sorry about your grandmother," Carter said, and he meant it. Being killed by someone you were trying to help sucked, and he should know. He'd lost too many brothers in blue because of that sort of thing, the most recent being Trooper Palmer.

"Thanks, but that was long before I was born. My

mother was just a little girl when that happened." They rounded the corner and the courthouse came into view. "Now isn't that pretty?" she asked as she pointed to it, and they watched as the automatic lights snapped on in the growing dusk.

"It is." A tiny voice whispered in his head, *Take her hand*, but he knew that wouldn't fly. When they reached the fountain, he motioned and she sat down on the edge of the pool. As soon as he was seated, he turned to her, trying to find the words he wanted to say. "I have to tell you, I shouldn't be here. I shouldn't have paid for your dinner, and I shouldn't be sitting here with you now."

Her eyes closed slowly and she nodded, an air of defeat seeming to drag her shoulders downward. "I know. But I'm glad you did—you're doing—all those things. It's nice to have company, especially company as nice as you."

"The pleasure's been all mine," he assured her, and when she flattened her palms on the top of the wall to brace herself, he let one of his fall on top of one of hers. "This has been the best evening I've spent in a long, long time."

"Me too." Her cheeks pinked, and all of a sudden, Carter felt very bold.

"So, if I asked you out, would you go?"

Her head snapped up and her lips pursed, but there was a curiosity in her eyes that took him by surprise. "I dunno. Are you interested in asking me out?"

Go for broke, Melton, he told himself. "Actually, yeah.

I am." Before she had a chance to say anything more, he added, "Are you the least bit attracted to me?"

"Wuhhhh, yeah. Absolutely. You're a very good-looking guy. But I bet you hear that all the time."

Carter laughed. "Nope! Can't say I've ever heard that!"

"I don't believe you."

"It's true. No woman has ever said that to me before, and especially not a beautiful woman like you." The instant the words were out, he wished he hadn't said them, but he was thrilled to see her cheeks go from a pale pink to a rosy blush.

"Sheriff—"

"Carter. My name's Carter."

She stopped and for a second or two, Carter thought he'd totally fucked up. But when she started again, her voice was different, lilting and light. "Carter. That's a nice name. Mine's Sharla. But you already know that."

"Yeah." He ran his fingers through his thick, dark hair, hoping he didn't have a cowlick sticking up in the back. God, he needed a haircut, but there never seemed to be time. It would've been nice if he'd had time before that particular moment. He'd always been careful about his appearance, but something about her made him want to clean up his act and buy a couple of pairs of new jeans and a new shirt or two. Being nervous around a woman was a new thing for him, but he was flustered in her presence. He hoped his voice wasn't too shaky when he said, "I guess I should call you that, huh? I've never known anybody by that name."

The twilight made the shadows of her face seem mysterious and brooding, and that wasn't what he'd seen in the warm light of the bar. A sudden urge hit him, an urge to take her somewhere where the light was golden and the air was filled with the smell of burgers grilling and coffee brewing. Before he had a chance to speak, her soft voice said, "I suppose I should get back. Morning comes early."

Just like that, the spell was broken. "Oh. Yeah, well, it does, doesn't it? Want a cup of coffee before you leave?"

She cocked her head and grinned at him. "You don't want this to end, do you?"

"Honestly?" She nodded in response. "No. No, I don't."

"Neither do I. Come on. I'm game for that coffee if you are."

Holy shit, Carter! She's really interested! For the first time since Mandy, Carter felt some sense of hope. Sharla Barker was beautiful, smart, and hardworking, all things he'd want in a woman. They rose and headed down the sidewalk in the direction of the bar, but he decided halfway down the block to take a chance and reached out, his right hand brushing her left one.

And just like that, her fingers wound into his and their palms met. Something coursed through Carter's body, some kind of energy that was unfamiliar but welcome, and his skin tingled. When his eyes darted to the side to catch a glimpse of her, he caught her doing the same to him, then dropping her gaze and grinning.

At the bar's door, he dropped her hand and held the door for her, then followed her to a table by the wall. He managed to catch the gaze of the bartender, mouthed the word *coffee*, and got a nod in reply. "So are you still coming to my house tomorrow evening?" she asked as he faced her again.

"Yeah. I need to talk to Chelsea and Lionel. Have you told them I'm coming?"

"No."

"Then please, don't. I wouldn't say I want this to be a surprise attack, but I want to catch them fresh. I don't want them all worked up from thinking about me being there. Does that make sense?"

"Sure. Mum's the word," she said in agreement as she smiled at the delivery of their coffee to the table. "Is it okay if I get all worked up from thinking about you being there?"

Carter gave a little chortle. "Sure! I'd be flattered."

"Good." Her hands were delicate with long, beautiful fingers, and he watched them caress the stem of the spoon, wishing it were a part of him that needed a woman's attention. She stirred the coffee slowly. "This has been nice."

"It has." He knew he needed to say something else, but he wasn't sure what. If Mac, his trainer back at the academy all those years before, could see him sitting there talking to a woman who was part of an investigation he was actively pursuing, the old man would have a fit. For some reason, Carter didn't care. There was something about Sharla Barker that really drew him in, and he wanted to find out exactly what that was. And if it was warm, pink, and wet? Well, all the better.

"I suppose I should get home. I need to do some laundry before they roll in tomorrow. And there's the matter of a funeral to plan too." Her voice was suddenly sad, and that made Carter sad too. He wished he could rewind everything that had happened, but there was no way to do that.

"I'll walk you to your car," he offered, then waited as she rose and followed her outside.

She turned at the corner of the building and meandered across the parking lot next door, Carter right behind her. When they reached her car, she stopped and fished out her keys before she said, "I guess I'll see you tomorrow evening?"

"Yeah. I don't know what time. It'll depend on what's going on. Can you help me out just a little and let me know when they get in?"

"Sure. The sooner we have all this unpleasantry behind us, the better for all of us. It's hard to feel good about seeing you tomorrow night when I know why you'll be there." No sooner had the words left her lips than she leaned in and gave Carter a light kiss on the cheek. No way had he seen that coming. Before he could speak, she said, "But I'll find a way to look forward to it. Goodnight, Carter."

Heat spread from his cheeks down his chest, and the lawman's heart beat wildly. "Goodnight, Sharla. See you tomorrow night." He stood there until she was locked into her car and her seatbelt was buckled, then made his way back to the sidewalk. As she pulled out of the parking lot, she tapped the horn and he turned to wave back.

Suddenly, the next evening's unpleasant task didn't seem quite so unpleasant. And if there was anything Carter Melton appreciated, it was a woman who knew exactly what she wanted. Unless he missed his guess, she wanted him, and he was pretty damn happy about that.

CHAPTER 3

WAS it wrong that he was looking forward to grilling a couple of young people about their sister and cousin's death? Maybe. But he was.

The day dragged on and on, and Carter didn't think it would ever be over. He contemplated staying in uniform—after all, it was an official interview—then said screw it and changed into jeans. Before he put on a tee, though, he reconsidered and pulled out a polo with the department's crest on it. One quick look in the mirror told him he most definitely needed a haircut, but there wasn't time for that, at least not before going to Sharla's house.

When she hadn't called by six, he decided he'd better get something to eat. It was nearing seven when his phone's text tone went off, and he checked it. Short, sweet, and to the point: *They just walked in. Anytime is fine.*

Eleven minutes later, he was standing at the front

door of a modest bungalow in one of the middle-class neighborhoods in Hopkinsville. Before he even had a chance to ring the doorbell, the door opened. There was a huge smile on her face when she breathed out, "Hey!"

"Hi. Thanks for texting me. Think they're ready?"

She shrugged. "Who knows? Come on in and I guess we'll find out." He let her lead him through the house to a small den on the back. "Just have a seat. Want something to drink? I've got fresh coffee?"

"Yeah. That sounds great. Thanks."

"Here you go," she said when she returned and set the mug down on the coffee table. "Sugar? Milk? Creamer?"

"No. Black is fine, thanks."

"Ready?"

"When you are."

"Kids? Could you come out into the den for a minute please?" Sharla called, and in seconds Carter could hear feet shuffling until two young faces appeared in the doorway. "Sheriff Melton's here and he wants to talk to you."

"I thought we didn't do anything wrong," Chelsea said barely over a whisper.

"You haven't. I just wanted to talk to you about Tamara, see if we could figure out what was going on. There are a lot of questions going unanswered, and we need to get to the bottom of all this." He motioned to the sofa across from him, and Chelsea and Lionel took a seat. Reaching into his pocket, he pulled out his phone, found the voice recorder, started it, and laid the phone on the table in front of the kids. "First, I haven't gotten a chance to talk to you, young man. I'm sorry about your sister."

"I heard it was you who shot her," the boy said, an edge to his voice but his expression flat.

"Actually, there were seven gunshot wounds, but it's true—mine was the one that did the deed. For that, I'm sorry, but she drew on us and we weren't left with a lot of options." He watched Lionel's face but the young man didn't appear to be confrontational, just trying to sort things out. Carter felt sorry for him. He was bound to be confused. "As I said, we've got some questions. First, how long had you been at the event when you left?"

Lionel and Chelsea glanced at each other. "Maybe two hours?" Chelsea answered, and Lionel nodded in agreement.

"And in that time, what did you do?"

"We just hung out and listened to the speakers," Lionel offered.

"Did you eat or drink anything?"

"I think I had a soda and some chips, and I remember you had a soda and some kind of food, right?" Chelsea said as she turned to Lionel.

"Yeah. A hot dog," the boy said with a nod.

"Did Tamara have anything?"

"Yeah," Chelsea answered. "She had a beer. At least one. Maybe two."

"Bottle? Can? Draft?"

Lionel answered, "In a cup. From a keg."

"And who was passing out the beer?"

They both shrugged before Chelsea said, "I dunno. Some volunteers, I think."

"And when did you observe Tamara acting strangely?"

They both sat for a few seconds, seemingly deep in thought, before Chelsea asked Lionel, "How long had we been there when that guy got up to speak? The one who was talking about the importance of taking what you want by force if necessary?"

"I don't know, but we left when he was finished."

"And that's when you observed her acting strangely?"

Chelsea nodded. "Yeah. Well, more like we said we wanted to leave because we were uncomfortable with the way the guy was talking, but she got mad because we didn't want to stay."

"Yeah, she got all huffy and asked us if we wanted somebody to hurt her and for her to be unable to defend herself. That's when she showed me her gun. I was ready to go then—I was totally freaked out by that," Lionel said, his eyes wide and eyebrows raised.

"And where did you go when you left there?" Carter asked.

"It was getting late, so we were going to come on home." Chelsea fiddled with the hem of her tee shirt. "I told her I'd drive because I didn't really think she should. Of course, I wasn't going to tell her that because she was acting so weird, but she insisted she wanted to."

"Weird how?"

"Really jumpy. Nervous. Kind of aggressive. Was that what you thought, Lionel?"

The young man nodded. "Yeah. Kind of aggressive. Very unlike her. Almost like we were the enemy."

"Uh, yeah. I think that's understandable," Carter said and waited for a response. Sure enough, both young people's brows furrowed in confusion. "What kind of drugs did you guys take?"

"We didn't take any drugs! I don't do that shi … stuff!" Chelsea fired back.

"Me either! I've gotta keep my GPA up or I lose my scholarship and I'd have to quit school!" Lionel cried out.

"Did you know Tamara had several different kinds of very dangerous drugs in her system?" Chelsea and Lionel's mouths dropped open and Carter could tell they weren't faking it—they had no idea Tamara had been under the influence. "Yeah. MDVP for one."

Lionel's voice was a breathy gasp. "Bath salts?"

"You know about them?"

"Yeah, everybody does. But Tamara would never do that stuff."

"There was also cocaine in her system." The kids turned to each other, their eyebrows disappearing into their hairlines and their mouths open in astonishment. "And Adderall. The ADHD drug?"

"Holy shit! All three?" Chelsea croaked.

"Yeah. All three. She was really out there when she was shot, and she'd been like that for a while, apparently."

"But those drugs don't last that long in the bloodstream. I know. I'm pre-med," Lionel pointed out.

"Well, there's the rub of it. Do either of you know anything about this?" Carter asked as he took out the picture of the tattoo and showed it to the kids.

Chelsea rolled her eyes. "Yeah. We know. I told her not to do it, but she did."

"So you know about the tattoo?"

"Oh, yeah. They were pushing people to get them," Lionel offered.

"They? Who's they?"

"The organizers of the event. The coordinators of the group that put it on," the young man said.

"Why?"

"Solidarity, they said," Lionel answered.

"And the bandage over it?"

Chelsea shrugged. "There were some guys walking through the crowd, asking if anybody had one of their tattoos. He said to put it on over the tattoo in case the cops showed up. It would make it hard for them to identify the members of the group, seeing as how they were telling all of us that the cops were out to get us."

"And the only people they were giving them to were people who had the tattoos?" Chelsea nodded. *Should I tell them about the bandages? Nah*, Carter decided. He'd save that piece of info in case he needed it. "And she took one and put it on?"

"Yeah," Lionel said.

"Did you notice anybody else acting weird?"

Chelsea shrugged. "I dunno. We didn't know any of those people, so there was no way of knowing how they usually acted. But I do know that as the event went on, people started getting crazier and louder. Don't you think so, Lionel?"

"Yeah. I noticed that. It was another reason why I wanted to leave. It started getting really loud, and I hate that."

"So back to the tattoo. Do you know what it means?"

Chelsea nodded. "Well, yeah. It's their logo."

"The organization? What's it called?"

Chelsea quirked an eyebrow up and scowled. "Um, tanner de lupo, I think? I don't know what that means." Suddenly, her gaze locked with Carter's. "Do you?"

"No. Can't say that I do, but I'm going to see if I can find out. In the meantime, I'd like for both of you to come down and look at some pictures to see if you can identify the guys who were speaking."

Lionel's face fell and his eyes misted over. "But my sister's funeral—"

"No rush. It can wait until afterward. But I can tell you that the longer we wait, the longer it will take to possibly figure out what was going on there and with Tamara. You do want your sister's death to make sense, don't you? Or the people who set this whole thing up to pay for their crime?"

"I do." Carter watched as the boy broke down and

his cousin wrapped her arm around his shoulder. "May I be excused? I need to go get ready. Coach Beckett said they'd do a little memorial for Tamara tonight at nine," he said, his voice soft and halting.

"Sure. We can take this up another time. Go. I'm glad they're doing that for her, and for you. And thank you for answering my questions. Get back to me when you're feeling better, okay?"

"Thank you," Chelsea whispered and smiled. "I know you're just trying to help, and we appreciate it, really."

"You're welcome. Now scoot." He watched as both kids rose and headed down the hallway, then turned to Sharla. "Good kids. This is such a shame."

"Think you got anything you can use?" she asked.

"I think it's important that I figure out this tanner de lupo thing."

"You really don't know what that means? Or you don't want them to—"

"No. I really don't know what that means, but I'm going to do some asking around. Maybe the guys who went to the university the day after the shooting found something. I dunno. It may be nothing. Or it may be something. But I do know something isn't right about this whole organization."

"I agree. Got anywhere you need to be?"

Carter smiled. "Nope. Not right now anyway."

"Good. Stick around and pretend you're going to ask me a bunch of questions." With that, Sharla rose and headed to the kitchen. When she reached the doorway, she spun and smiled. "More coffee, sheriff?"

"Don't mind if I do!" Carter grabbed his mug and decided he'd go that direction instead of waiting for her. Just like the rest of the house, the kitchen was nondescript, its floor covering worn and plain and its curtains faded. Everything was clean, but there was nothing new in the room, and he was pretty sure the refrigerator was a breath away from taking a shit. There wasn't a lot of money floating around there, that much was obvious. That was the moment something crossed his mind, something he'd wondered about but forgotten to ask. "Hey, Sharla, about Tamara's funeral on Sunday ..."

"Yeah?" she answered, never turning to look at him as she cut a piece of Danish sitting on the counter.

"Did you have life insurance for—"

"No. I'm not sure how I'm going to pay for it, but I will."

"The department has a fund. I could talk to them and—"

"That's not necessary."

"I insist." Carter reached for his mug, refilled and steaming, and when he grabbed it, their fingers touched for an instant.

He felt like he'd been struck by lightning. The hair on the back of his neck rose and gooseflesh popped up on his arms. His first thought was to wonder how long the kids would be gone to the memorial service, and he chastised himself immediately for thinking that way

49

when the family was in mourning. But he couldn't help it. When their eyes met, she smiled, and he wondered if she'd felt it too. She'd been coming onto him ever since the evening before, and he had to wonder what she thought was going to happen between them. He had no idea what that would be, but he knew what he *wanted* it to be.

He wanted to fuck her silly. Right that second. In that moment, it became his number one goal in life, and he was rabid about meeting his goals.

"You okay?" Her soft voice brought him out of his thoughts and he almost choked.

"Yeah. Fine. Good coffee," he answered and took a sip, hoping his hands weren't shaking too hard.

"Good company," she responded with a wink that almost made him come undone. He chided himself for his lack of self-control and, in the same internal breath, congratulated himself for wearing jeans. At least the hardness straining against his fly was a little more disguised than it would've been in his uniform slacks.

"Mom?" a voice called out, and Carter almost dropped his coffee. Could the kids figure out what he was thinking? Had he looked at Sharla in a way that would tip them off? God, he hoped not.

"Yes, baby. You guys ready to go?"

"Yes, ma'am. We'll be back around midnight, I suppose. They want to have the service and then have a little reception. I'm sure there'll be all kinds of food and all the teachers will want to talk to us, so it'll be late." Carter watched as Chelsea pulled on a thin cardigan while Lionel carried a lightweight jacket.

"That's fine. Please call me when you're on your way so I'll know to be watching for you."

"You don't have to wait up, Mom. You need to go to bed. You've got work in the morning and—"

"I'm your mom. I'll always worry—even more now. Go. Tell them I said thanks for doing this and I'd come but I'm just too tired. Sheriff Melton wants to ask me some questions, so I'm just going to hang out here."

"Okay. We'll call on our way back. Bye," Chelsea called back into the house.

"Bye, Auntie Sharla. Thanks, Sheriff Melton," Lionel added.

"You're welcome, son," Carter replied. "Drive safely." The door closed behind the kids and in a few seconds, Carter could hear the car start and the sound of its tires on the pavement as it pulled away from the curb. "That's nice of the teachers to do that for them."

"It is. We've got a great community here. Everybody's taking this really hard." Sharla took a sip of her coffee and set her mug down. "And there's something I wanted to tell you."

Please, god, let it be that she wants me to bang her, Carter's brain whispered to him, hardening his cock even more. "Yeah?"

"I'm pretty sure somebody followed me home last night."

That wasn't at all what he'd thought she was going to say. "What? Are you sure?"

51

"No. Not a hundred percent. But I'm pretty sure. I took a couple of turns to see what would happen, and they stayed right on me."

"Why didn't you call me?" he whisper-shouted.

"Because I wasn't totally positive and I didn't want to be the boy who cried wolf. But it shook me up a bit." She wasn't lying—her face had paled enough that it was noticeable in the mediocre kitchen lighting.

"Can you think of a reason anybody would have to do that?"

"Like …"

"Like has anybody been harassing you at work? Creepy guy hanging around? Anything amiss around here, like graffiti on the house or car, or your garbage can being gone through? Anybody threatening you because of what Tamara did?"

"No. I can't think of anything. There's no reason for anybody to follow me."

Carter stood there for a minute, trying to figure out what to do. He didn't want to alarm her, but he wanted her safe. "If you notice anything like that again, call me while it's happening and keep driving. I'll get in touch with the Hopkinsville police and have them intercept you and follow them. I …" Did he want to say it? "I don't want anything to happen to you."

"I'm sure I'm just being paranoid—"

"I don't think so. If you think they were following you, they probably were. Promise me you'll call me. Sharla? I mean it. Promise."

"Okay! I will, I will!" Her voice softened as she said, "I just don't want to bother you."

"You're no bother, you or the kids. I kinda want to see where this thing goes, okay?"

"Yeah. Me too."

Go for broke, Carter, he told himself. "Look, I'd love to take you to dinner, but I don't think that would be a good idea, at least not until the investigation is over. But when it is—"

A sly smile pulled up the corners of her mouth. "You don't have to wine and dine me, Carter. That's not necessary. We can skip the formalities. I'd be just as happy with an evening at your house."

Carter gave a little chuckle. "I think that can be arranged! Let me know if you know when the kids will be gone. Maybe we can plan something."

"They're gone now ..." There was no time to respond before she stepped up to him and pressed her lips to his.

That was all the invitation he needed, and he pressed his palms to her cheeks, holding her face to his, his thumbs stroking her cheekbones. A sound rose from her throat, a low growl that made her lips vibrate against his and set him on fire. God, she was a vixen, slutty enough to excite him and sweet enough to make him want to protect her. When he broke the kiss and leaned back, he gave her a lazy smile that he hoped translated into lust. "Bedroom?"

"No. Here." Sharla leaned in and her lips tickled his earlobe when she whispered, "Fuck me here."

It took him two seconds flat to lift her to perch on the edge of the kitchen table, and by the time he dragged her panties down, he was so hard that he could barely squat to pull off her shoes and rid her of everything below her waist. He started to thank her for wearing a dress to make things easier when he realized she'd planned the whole thing. She wanted him. God, that was so fucking awesome. Most women ran away from him. Nobody wanted to be a cop's girlfriend or wife, but this woman seemed to have no problem with it. When he rose back to his feet, she grabbed his belt and unbuckled it, then worked on the button of his jeans, followed by his zipper. Her fingers were mesmerizing, and he watched them, his eyes hungry to see his own hard manhood, to know it was ready to take her and give her what she'd obviously been thinking about ever since the night before. No waiting—he unceremoniously thrust two fingers into her pussy and smiled at the wetness he found there. "Been thinking about this long?" he asked, grinning at her.

"Ever since you walked into the bar last night. I almost asked you to fuck me in the back seat of my car."

"You need to know that women never come onto me like this," Carter said, slipping his fingers out of her, holding them in front of her face, and licking them slowly to watch her squirm.

She let out a little laugh, a chirpy little thing that made his heart quiver. "I don't understand that. Men in uniform are sexy as hell."

He pressed his jeans and boxer briefs downward until his steely shaft sprang free, and he groaned as her hand wrapped around it. "I'm not wearing a uniform," he pointed out.

"You were the first time I met you," she argued, her hand sliding up and down his length. Her strokes were solid and she was gripping him tightly enough to fill his vision with stars. "Do you want me, Carter?"

"I do." He attacked her mouth, his tongue stroking into hers, lashing against her tongue, hands roaming her body until he found the zipper on the front of her dress and pulled it downward. To his delight, she was wearing a front-clasped bra, and he snapped it apart, ran his hands across the top of her collarbone, and pressed her dress and bra straps backward.

His reward was two full, heavy breasts, their hard, dark nipples pointing slightly upward. A college buddy had taught him something that he'd never forgotten: *Stare at a woman's tits. If you stare long enough, it embarrasses her a little, and that makes it easier to fuck her. An embarrassed woman will want to please you. It works, Carter, trust me.* It always had. To his surprise, as he stared, she squeezed her shoulder blades together and thrust her breasts forward. "Like what you see?" she asked, her tone haughty, and Carter was impressed. She wasn't the least bit embarrassed. Matter of fact, she seemed proud.

"Oh, yeah. Beautiful. Can't wait to suck 'em," he said, kissing her again. "Nip 'em," he added as he nuzzled the side of her neck. "Pull 'em," he whispered against her collarbone. "Twist 'em." He let his tongue slide from her collarbone down the gentle slope toward her nipple and listened to her breath hitch. His lips were almost to them when she said something that set him on fire.

"Hurt 'em. I like it rough."

JACKPOT! Carter wanted to scream. Holy hell, he had a live one! His lips locked around her left nipple and he sucked hard, his left hand reaching for the right one, gripping it, and pulling hard before twisting it viciously. The breath she sucked in between her barely-parted lips made his cock throb. Yes—this was exactly what he wanted, and he wanted it right that minute. His teeth latched around her hardened nub and hung on as he righted himself, and she hissed and leaned back as her flesh stretched. When he couldn't pull upward any farther without doing her injury, he let go just to watch her breast drop and bounce, then stared into her eyes. "I don't think you like it as rough as I'd like to give it to you."

"Try me." There was a challenge in that statement, one that Carter couldn't ignore. And then he thought of something that made him groan.

"Shit. I don't have a condom."

"You fuck around?"

"Hell no. I don't have time."

Sharla giggled. "Well, neither do I. I haven't been with anybody in four years."

"It's been almost two for me. I guess we don't have much to worry about, now do we?" he asked as he pressed his lips to hers again and felt her fingers dig into his ass, drawing him closer, begging him to enter her.

Begging wasn't necessary. Carter thrust himself into her, burying his length inside her warmth and darkness, and the cry she let loose made him feel like a superhero. He dragged her right to the edge of the table, his arms under her legs, hands gripping her ass, and slammed into her like an ax into firewood. "Jesus, Carter, fuck me!" she yelled and leaned back, resting her elbows on the table, her upper body on full display and those mighty tits rolling up and down. Leaning in, he trapped her right nipple in his teeth and gave a hard nip. "Shit! Oh, yeah! Um-hmmm. Oh, baby, fuck me. Fuck me, sheriff. Oh, yeah, fuck me," she ordered, almost yelling. Could the neighbors hear her? He hoped like hell they could.

God, he felt alive! Everything else melted away as he pounded into her, and there was only him and her and his hard cock moving in and out of her tight, hot pussy. Was anything else necessary? No. Was anything else any more important? Hell no. She vacillated between screaming, swearing, whimpering, begging, and moaning, and the noise alone was enough to get him off. She wrapped her legs around his waist and as he stroked into her, her legs dangled, her heels occasionally smacking him in the small of the back. He was about to ask her how she was liking it when she bent forward, wrapped her hands around his neck, and pulled herself up to kiss him.

He wanted to give her more—he really did—but it had been so long and she felt so good against him and around him that he couldn't hold off. There was no way she could be any more disappointed in him than he was in himself as his body let go and he filled her with stickiness. "Shit," he muttered against her lips, as irritated as he'd been in a long time. God damn it, he felt like a fourteen-year-old school boy.

"What?" she whispered into his neck.

"I didn't intend to—"

"Hey." Forcing himself to focus, he looked down into her face and saw her smiling up at him. "I was good enough that you couldn't hold off. That makes me feel like a fairy princess, buddy. I'm about as sexy as a pair of orthopedic loafers. You losing it like that? Quite the ego boost for me," she said, chuckling under her breath. Carter couldn't help it—he started to laugh. "What? You think I'm kidding?"

He leaned forward until she was flat on the table under him, his softening manhood still inside her. "You are ridiculously sexy, woman. Don't you know that?"

"Me? Stop trying to make me feel better," she said with a snort, and Carter finally understood. She meant what she was saying. She didn't think she was appealing at all. What the hell?

"Are you kidding? I mean, Jesus, girl, you're hot and tight and those tits … I mean, those things … You should win some kind of award or something. They're, well, magnificent is the first word that comes to mind."

Her eyes went round and her eyebrows arched. "You're kidding, right?"

"Kidding? Hell no, I'm not kidding. My only regret is that I didn't get a really good look at that ass, but if it's as fine as those tits, then my god, if we do this again I'm only going to last a couple of minutes every time. I won't be able to hold off. You'll just suck the life outta my man bone down there, baby."

She started laughing, and he had to admit he liked it. With every chortle, she tightened around him, and he could feel his softness turning hard again. But there was something even more important going on there.

He was having fun. She was *fun*. There was a light-heartedness, a gleefulness, about it that he'd never had before with sex. He wanted to do it again, not because it felt so damn good, which it did, but because it was fun. For the first time ever, he wasn't concentrating on the act just as a performance, but as a pleasure. They were playing around. She was smiling and laughing, and so was he.

It hit him like a runaway freight train—this was what he wanted, a relationship with another grownup where they had grownup sex and acted like grownups about it. Sex that didn't feel like a business contract. Sex that wasn't solemn or stiff or stuffy. Fun sex, sex where they laughed and whispered and talked about what they were doing with and to each other, and nobody was embarrassed. He liked it. And he wanted more.

Almost as though she could read his mind, she said,

"*Now* let's go to the bedroom. Come on." Pushing him back until he broke free from her, she took his hands, dropped to the floor, and strolled off toward the bedroom, pulling him along as he struggled to keep up with his jeans and briefs still around his thighs. He was sure he looked ridiculous and he didn't care. Matter of fact, he was almost laughing about it by the time they reached the bedroom.

But when they reached the bedroom, he breathed a sigh of pure bliss as he watched her turn her back to him, lift up her dress, and pull it up over her head and off. Sure enough, her ass was a beautiful heart-shaped thing, sloping just perfectly to curl up and join her thighs, and when she turned, naked and silent, toward him, he thought he'd never seen anything so beautiful in his life. The polo shirt came up and off over his head and as soon as he'd dropped his briefs and jeans, Sharla stepped up and ran a hand from his waist up his chest, threading her fingers through the dark hair there, until her hand reached his chin. She gripped it with a forefinger and thumb and smiled. "God, look at you," she whispered up to him, a sly smile splitting her face. "All man. Muscles, dark hair, golden skin. Jesus, Carter, you could be a model, you know that?"

"Me? Nah. I'm just an ordinary Joe," he whispered back and kissed her forehead.

"You're a lot of things, but you're not ordinary. You're extraordinary." Then she rose up on her tiptoes and softly swept her lips across his.

It took little more than an instant for Carter to lay

her out on the bed and slide down her body. God, she smelled amazing, a heady mixture of soap, perfume, and arousal all rolled together to make his mouth water. Tonguing the nub he sought out in her slit, he sucked in a breath as she tugged his hair and flexed his hips ever so slightly to rub his hardening cock against the sheets. He wanted to fuck her right that minute, but he'd already decided she had to come. No way would he let her go unsatisfied again. As he concentrated on teasing her, he held her hips down so she couldn't thrust and delighted in her cries of exasperation as her arousal increased. She was getting closer, closer, so much closer, and he stopped just long enough to crawl up between her thighs, rise up on his knees, and bury himself in her pussy. When he was deep inside her, he pressed down on her belly while his right index finger and thumb opened her slit and exposed her swollen clit to the air.

She cried out as he started to stroke. Watching her was amazing. Her hands roamed her own body, and he couldn't believe how painfully arousing it was to watch her fondle her own nipples, pulling and tugging and twisting them. "God, babe," he whispered down to her, "watching you ... I wanna fuck you so hard."

"Fuck me, Carter. I want you to fuck me over and over. Fuck me 'til I can't walk. I mean it. Own me. Make me your slut."

No woman had ever talked to him that way during sex, and he loved it. Jesus, she made him ache! As she struggled to keep her climax at bay, he could feel her clenching and releasing around his cock, and he prayed she'd come soon so he could stroke into her. His hardness burned and throbbed, and he needed relief. She had to know that was what he was waiting for, and she didn't seem to care. Or maybe she was teasing him. All he knew was that she was twitching and jerking all over, trying so hard to hold off, and all he really wanted was to feel her convulse around him.

And then she did. Her back arched, her fingers pulled her nipples out impossibly far, and she shrieked as the muscles in her belly rolled and twitched. "That's it, baby. Come hard for me, girl. Ohhhh, my god, I've gotta fuck you. I can't wait anymore." As soon as his hand left her clit, he gripped her waist with both hands and banged into her.

Watching his cock move in and out of her was like an Oscar-winning film to Carter. His shaft glistened with her juices, and all he could think about was the next stroke. Listening to her crying out and begging him to fuck her was just the icing on the cake. He could feel himself getting closer, and when he pressed his hands to the back sides of her thighs and bent her double with her knees to her chest, she opened like a flower and he could see it all, every sacred inch of her femininity, every pink, hot, wet centimeter she had to offer. Still pressing her thighs downward, he pulled them together too, trapping her breasts between them to watch their fullness, making her tighter, so tight that he could barely breathe. Carter threw his head back, closed his eyes, and fucked her. He fucked her like he'd never fucked another woman, like she was the last woman on earth and he was going to wear that thing out. His balls ached. His shaft burned. He was a fucking machine, and this woman was taking it and giving it back to him in spades.

When he emptied into her, he felt like he'd single-handedly won the third world war or found the cure for the common cold or solved the problem of global hunger. He was powerful and invincible. His cock was throbbing and it hurt so damn good. By the time he caught his breath, he realized he hadn't even taken a moment to check on her.

But he needn't have worried. Sharla lay there, smiling up at him, and he felt a catch in his chest. *Oh, shit, I'm so royally fucked*, he told himself, because he knew the truth. He didn't want this to be a fling, not something that was a two- or three-time deal and then he'd walk away. No, this was something he hadn't had before, with a woman the likes of whom he'd never known before. Sharla Barker was the kind of woman he'd been looking for all along and never thought he'd find. "You okay, babe?" he asked as he gazed down at her, his dick still buried in her and her knees still up, legs wide open, and everything between her thighs wet.

"Yeah. I'm fine. And you look fucking hot kneeling between my legs like that, Carter. I mean, really. You're such a fucking stud, babe."

He couldn't help it—he threw his head back and laughed. It wasn't because what she'd said was funny, even though it was. It was from pure relief. My god, what a feeling! Pulling out of her, he dropped to the mattress beside her and pulled her up against him, his arms tight around her. "I bet you say that to all the sheriffs, don't you?"

"Only the cute ones." She kissed his chin lightly and his whole body warmed. When she burrowed her head into the side of his neck, he knew what it felt like to be a man. She didn't know it yet, but Sharla Barker was going to be his. He wasn't letting go. "How long can you stay?"

"Well, we know I have to be gone by the time the kids get back. What time is it?"

"It's almost eleven."

Carter pulled back and stared down at her in disbelief. "We've been fucking for *two hours?*"

Sharla laughed heartily. "Looks like it!"

"God, woman, it's a miracle I'm not dead!" he barked, laughing with her.

"I know, right? I'm trying to wear you out. Is it working?"

He chuckled and kissed the top of her head. "No. I'm just getting started."

"Good. I don't want it to stop. Well, I mean, I know it has to stop tonight. I mean I don't want it to stop ever. Wait—I don't mean ever as in forever, I mean—"

"Shush. I know what you mean. It's fine. I don't want it to ever stop either." Throwing his free arm up, he lay back on the pillow, his other arm cradling her against his body, and smiled up at the ceiling. Her skin against his was warm and soft, and he loved the sensation of her breath as it floated across his chest. If only they had all night ...

"Carter?"

"Yeah?"

"Thanks."

He ran his fingers through her hair and kissed her forehead before he asked, "For what?"

She let out a little sigh. "For helping me forget for just a little while."

That struck him as profoundly sad. "You're welcome but, honestly, I hope it was more than that."

"Oh, it is. But this week ... I feel like I've been dropped into hell. I don't know what to do next, and everything is upside down, and—"

"Stop. It's okay. Just take a deep breath. You've got to get through the funeral somehow, I know, and then hopefully it'll get better."

He felt her shift, and she threw an elbow across his chest, her hand resting on his collar bone as she stared into his face. "Are you coming to the funeral?"

"Under the circumstances, I think it would be awkward for everybody involved, don't you?"

"The kids and I would like for you to be there."

"But Sharla, it was my bullet that—"

"If we don't mind, nobody else should." He was about to speak when she added, "Unless it would make you too uncomfortable."

He closed his eyes and shook his head. "It's not about my comfort or discomfort. I'll do whatever you want me to, whatever would make you and the kids most comfortable."

"We'd like for you to be there."

"Well, I guess that settles it. I'll be there. Just make sure I know what time."

"Okay. Thanks." Her head dropped onto his shoulder as her hand glided across his midsection, coming to rest on the side of his ribcage. Without a second thought, his free hand draped across her and he pulled her in even tighter to his side.

If she and the kids wanted him there, he'd be there. Yeah, he'd have to answer a bunch of questions from people whose business it was *not*, but that was okay. His only concern was the trouble it might cause them. And if it caused them any, he'd take care of that too.

CHAPTER 4

It was the perfect time for some digging. Saturday mornings were quiet at the office. They ran a skeleton crew of only the officers they needed, all out on the road. Carter got up a little earlier than usual and headed in. As he unlocked the door, he noticed Watson and Durst's vehicles sitting there, so it was a sure thing they were out and about.

He brought up the computer on his desk and logged in. Then he went through his email. Nothing important. After that, he started prowling through databases.

Sharla LeAnne Meacham Barker. Carter checked every record he could think of and found nothing—not so much as a parking ticket. The woman was squeaky clean. Another quick check and he found nothing on the two kids. Matter of fact, there was nothing on Tamara either, but based on the things Sharla had said, that didn't surprise him.

He did a little backtracking and found the court

case with Tamara and Lionel's father. It appeared Taliq Lamar Kent had been a Grade A piece of shit. There were numerous records for domestic assault, and they weren't just against Sharla's sister, Imogen. It appeared he'd had several women on the side over the years, and he'd treated them as badly as he'd treated his wife. The robbery had gone sour from the very beginning—silent alarm set off almost immediately, getaway driver caught right around the corner, and the three inside the bank running out and straight into a wall of blue. Two of them had dropped to their faces, but not Taliq Kent. He'd pulled a forty-five and gotten himself blown to bits, just as his daughter had. For Tamara, her willingness to pull that gun had come from the knowledge she was going down for a crime. Based on the statements from the officers present, Taliq had simply been boasting about how he was going down in a blaze of glory. But Carter had to ask himself, *What role did her dad's death play in Tamara's decision to draw on us?* He had to wonder if there was some tiny thought in the back of her mind, some sad decision to let history repeat itself within their family. And what a shame that was.

He had to admit, he felt better about Sharla. All night long after he'd gone home, he'd lain awake, wondering if he'd messed up badly by getting involved with someone whose character was less than stellar. It seemed he'd worried for nothing. Sharla was exactly as she appeared to be.

But that tattoo wasn't. He pulled out his phone and

hit a contact. It only rang twice before a voice answered with, "Atkins."

"Good morning. This is Sheriff Melton over in Trigg County. How are you?"

"Doing good. You guys doing okay down there?"

"Yeah. Got a funeral to attend sometime next week."

"So I heard. You're actually going?"

"Yeah. The woman and kids have requested that I be there."

There was a brief hiccup of silence before Atkins said, "That's highly unusual."

"Not really," Carter threw back, trying to think fast. "I've been questioning them in regard to the case and I think they realize I just want the truth to come out so they can get some closure. They said they'd be more comfortable with me there."

"Well, you're a better man than I am. I don't think I could do it," Atkins announced.

"Thanks, but it's about their comfort. They're grieving. I feel like I owe them that, not to mention they might need security. Because of the nature of the crime, there may be people who'll blame the family, and I don't want anything to happen to them. But I just wondered: Did you find out anything at the university?"

"Hang on. Let me grab my notes." Carter sat with the phone to his ear and listened as the sound of footsteps receded, then seemed to come back before he heard Atkins ask, "Still there?"

"Yeah."

"Okay. I interviewed the dean of students. He said the organization calls itself the Rainbow University League. Other than the name, he really doesn't know much about it."

"All of those organizations are supposed to have a sponsor who's a member of the faculty," Carter pointed out.

"Right. And it appears whoever their sponsor was retired two years ago. And that was just about the time the organization was formed. Get this—there wasn't another one assigned. It's like nobody thought to ask somebody else to be their sponsor, just kept feeding them the paperwork to stay on campus."

Carter could feel his eyebrows pop up. "That's pretty weird."

"Yeah. I thought so too. I talked to the woman over in Faculty Hall whose office is responsible for issuing the paperwork. She said she got it ready every year and gave it to the dean of curriculum to assign. And every year the dean signed it and gave it back. So nobody was addressing the fact that they had no sponsor. Looks like they slipped through the cracks."

"Or sneaked through the cracks. Maybe somebody knew they didn't have a sponsor and wanted to keep it that way," Carter mused aloud.

"I thought of that too, so I did some checking and if there's any infraction being perpetrated, or that has been perpetrated, by any of the faculty, I haven't found it. Of course, I know universities have a way of burying that stuff."

"True. So I assume you asked students around campus?"

"Duffy did that while I was talking with administration. He said it was as though the organization didn't exist. Nobody he stopped seemed to know anything about it. Matter of fact, he sat out in front of the library and watched for kids with gay pride shirts on or carrying anything that would give him reason to think they were gay. Found about eight of them in just a few minutes, and they all claimed to know nothing about the organization. I found that pretty strange."

"It is."

"So what did the two kids know?"

"Nothing," Carter answered, feeling more than frustrated. They were getting nowhere fast, it appeared. "The Kent girl was the one who initiated the attendance at the rally. Neither of them are gay, neither are members of the organization, and they know very little about it. Said it's called tanner de lupo?"

"Huh. Well, that's a new one on me. I haven't heard that. What does that mean?"

Carter shrugged to himself. "I have no idea, but I aim to find out. If I do, I'll let you guys know."

"Sounds good. Maybe you could get the kids to go to another one of those rallies," Atkins suggested.

"That's a good idea, but considering they didn't know anything about it and just went along with the Kent girl, I'd say their chances of finding out about another rally would be pretty slim unless somebody let it slip. But they *are* on campus and we're not, so I'll talk to them about keeping an ear to the ground."

"Sounds good. If I hear anything, I'll let you know," Atkins assured him.

"Thanks. Same here. Have a good weekend." Carter hit END and sat there. Nobody seemed to know anything. What would it take to find out? And how long?

If there really was somebody following Sharla, even one more day might be too long.

* * *

HE'D CHECKED ON SHARLA BOTH DAYS WITH A TEXT, AND she claimed she was fine. Carter wanted to see her, but with the kids home for the weekend, that just wasn't possible. Not that they'd be any kind of security, but at least she wasn't alone in the house. That was something.

He spent Sunday afternoon at his mom's, fixing her bathtub faucet and building some stairs to the little shed out back. It was beyond worth the effort when he discovered she'd spent the afternoon making chicken 'n dumplings from scratch, his grandmother's recipe and his absolute favorite meal. One thing Carter could honestly say was that he enjoyed spending time with his mom. He'd felt the same way about his dad, and he often thought of things he'd like to tell his father if only he were still alive. When the investigation was over and he and Sharla could see each other openly, he could see himself stepping into that role with Chelsea, if she'd let him. After all, she came with Sharla, so they'd have to get along.

Matter of fact, he'd been thinking about a relationship with the brunette beauty ever since they'd spent the evening together. Sharla was everything he'd ever wanted in a woman, insofar as he could tell. Of course, he needed to get to know her a lot better, but that wasn't going to happen until they could get the investigation settled.

So bright and early on Monday, when the call came, he was glad. "Sure. I'll be there."

"Two. Bring anything you've dredged up and we'll all talk about it," Griffin ordered.

"Will do, sir. See you then." *Finally—we're seeing some movement, even if I'm going to have to drive like a maniac to get there*, he told himself as he readied his messenger bag, pulling the files he'd started on Sharla, Lionel, Chelsea, and Tamara into it, along with some other information he'd found. Last but not least, he'd actually transcribed the notes he'd taken during the meeting he'd had with the kids the week before, and he took time to make copies of them so he'd have them to hand out.

He hit the road with enough time to stop in Bardstown on the way and grab a bite to eat. It was an easy-enough drive, parkways and interstates almost the entire way. One look at his uniform and the server at the restaurant got his food and got him out the door as quickly as possible. By the time he pulled into the parking lot at the state police headquarters in Frankfort, the state's capitol, he had forty-five minutes to spare.

There were handshakes and fresh coffee awaiting him as he walked in, and one of the clerks showed him to the conference room they'd be using. Bud Griffin was there, as were Ron Duffy and Jason Atkins. He hadn't seen Amos Fletcher and Jesse Talbert yet. A hand landed on his back between his shoulder blades and he turned to find Sam Curry standing there. "Hey, Sam!"

"Carter!" The men shook hands jovially, and Carter was glad to see Sam there. He'd felt a little out of place and outranked by the state police detectives and KDCI agents, but with Sam in attendance, at least he had another small-town guy participating.

They sat and chatted as they waited, mostly about Sam's two-year-old twin boys. It hurt Carter a little to hear about their antics. If he'd had a different job, or found someone when he was younger, or … There went that *if only* beratement again. Those years were lost and they weren't coming back. Might as well enjoy hearing about somebody else's little family.

There were ten minutes left in their wait when Fletcher and Talbert stepped into the room. Along with them came a man Carter didn't recognize, but all the KSP personnel seemed to know him. As the last one in, Bud closed the door behind himself and turned to the men. "Everyone stand and introduce yourself."

One by one, they stood and gave their name and

position. The unknown man's name was Marlon Waters, and he was a deputy state medical examiner, which made sense to Carter. As soon as they were finished with the introductions, they launched into the meeting.

Carter was surprised to find they really had very little information. Most surprising was how little Duffy and Atkins had managed to scare up on campus. They had nothing more than Carter had already heard.

Sam actually had some new information in the form of the tattoo artists who'd produced the tattoos, but unfortunately, it seemed every one of them generated no leads. They were college students doing internships with tattoo parlors, or long-time residents of the area who had no ties to campus whatsoever. "What did they say about the design?" Carter asked.

"That the kids brought them drawings of it. All they had to do was ink it on. They all wondered about it, especially when more kids came in wanting it, but they all said the same thing—the only questions they ask are about age for legal purposes. Otherwise, it's the client's body and the client's choice."

"So they have no idea what the tattoo is about?" Griffin asked.

Sam shook his head. "Nope."

Then it was Carter's turn. He pulled out the transcripts of the notes from his questioning of Chelsea and Lionel and watched Griffin's eyebrows shoot up. *No doubt he's surprised I'm so professional*, Carter thought, mentally rolling his eyes. The state police and KDCI often treated local sheriffs as though they were Barney Fife clones, but most of the sheriffs, sheriff's deputies, and sheriff's department detectives he knew were highly-trained, skilled, hard-working men and women who knew their jobs. "Take a look at that one section there, the one that's highlighted," Carter said, pointing to the paper. "According to the kids, the organization is called something like tanner de lupo. They have no idea what that means." Oddly, about the time the words came out of his mouth, he felt something under the table. Had Sam just kicked him? What the hell? He took a chance and glanced at the county detective, watching one of the man's eyebrows hike ever so slightly. Sam knew something, something he didn't want to share in the group. Suddenly, Carter couldn't wait for the meeting to be over so he could talk to Sam alone. "Ran it through five translation engines and got a mish mash of stuff, none of which made any sense. Anybody hear this from anybody else? Know what it means?" he asked aloud, half to see if he got an answer and half to smokescreen his connection with Sam. Everyone shrugged or shook their head. "Okay, then. I'm going to follow it, if that's okay with everybody else."

"Go for it," Bud answered, then pointed to the next participant.

By the time they finished, they had little more than when they'd started. Waters had answered several questions, mostly about drugs, and one of them was something Carter had thought of but hadn't had a chance to ask for. Had he analyzed the drugs he'd found in Tamara's system to see if they matched anything else he'd seen? His answer was yes, and he claimed he'd found a few that were close, but none that were identical to the composition. *Well, scratch that*, Carter thought.

In all, fifty-five minutes was all they spent, fifty-five minutes Carter felt he could've better spent in investigation, except for one thing—Sam. "You know where Dandy's Coffee is?" Sam asked off-handedly as they strode out of the building.

"Yep. See you there," Carter answered, being careful of the volume of his voice. He knew what was happening, and he didn't want anybody else figuring out what the two were up to.

They found a seat in the corner and waited until the barista finished their orders before they got down to business. Carter could barely wait. "Well?" Instead of speaking, Sam slid a piece of paper toward him with a phone number written on it. "What's this?"

"Guy my wife knows. You do realize Dahlia is former FBI," Sam said, taking a sip of his coffee.

"No shit? Had no idea! So who is this?"

"His name is Cruz Livingston. Down in San Antonio. I think you should talk to him. May be nothing; may be something."

"Like what?"

"Tanner de lupo. You do know what *lupo* means, right?" Carter shook his head. "Wolf."

"Wolf." What was tickling his brain?

"*Lupo* is Italian for 'wolf.' Who operates out of Texas?"

It hit Carter like a ton of bricks. "Los Lobos."

"Exactly."

Sour dread balled up in Carter's stomach. Los Lobos was a notorious Latino gang in Texas, spending the last twenty years branching out into every major U.S. city. They were the epitome of evil, spreading prostitution, drugs, illegal alcohol production, and worst of all, illegal firearms. Bump stocks were turning up for AR-15s all over the place, and most of them were being illegally distributed by Los Lobos. "What do you think this Livingston guy can tell me?"

"I know he did some undercover work for the FBI on some gang activity in the San Antonio area. He might be able to give you some info, or at least point you in the right direction."

"Why aren't you doing this and taking credit for it?" Carter asked. He'd been in law enforcement long enough to be suspicious.

"Because you were there when Palmer bled out. Because your bullet was the one … Because I'd like to see you catch a break on this one and show these troopers a thing or two. They look down their noses at us. You know it and I know it. And we need to get one up on them," Sam said from inside his coffee cup.

"And solve the case," Carter interjected.

"Most definitely solve the case. And listen, if I can help you with anything, anytime, never hesitate to ask.

And Sheriff Massey said that goes for our whole department." Massey was the sheriff in Calloway County, the department Sam worked for, and that was huge for Carter, having Calloway County not only cooperate with them but offer assistance.

"Thanks. I really appreciate that. Same goes for us, if we can ever help you."

"You're welcome, and thank you." Sam took the final swig of his coffee and set his cup down. "I've gotta get back, but call Livingston and see what he can tell you. Can't hurt."

"I will. Thanks again." Carter watched the detective turn and head out, thinking all the while how nice it was that *somebody* wanted to help him. They all treated the tiny county seat of Cadiz like it was nothing. But if he figured this out ...

He had to, for his reputation, for the good of his department, and for Trooper Palmer. And for Sharla, Chelsea, and Lionel.

* * *

Two beers. He was sufficiently loosened up, he figured, so he pulled out the slip of paper and dialed the number. It only rang twice before a male voice barked, "Yes?"

"I'm trying to reach Cruz Livingston."

"You've found him."

"This is Carter Melton. I'm the sheriff in Trigg County, Kentucky, and—"

"Sam! Yeah, he called and said he'd given you my number. Good to hear from you."

Wow, this guy isn't stuck up or short with me, Carter thought. He'd never thought anyone from the FBI would be willing to help him with anything. "Thanks. And thanks for talking to me."

"We should all cooperate with each other. So whaddya got?"

Carter launched into the information he'd been given, but when he said the words *tanner de lupo,* Cruz yelled, "Whoa! Stop right there. Tanner de lupo?"

"What?"

"Could it be *la tana del lupo?*"

"I suppose. That's just what the kids called it."

"Can you send me a pic of this tattoo you're telling me about?"

"Sure. I'll send it in a text while we're talking." Carter pulled the picture over, snapped a shot of it on his phone, then listened to the *swoosh* that told him the text was on its way to Cruz. "It should hit you in just a few seconds."

"Got it. Let me look." There was another brief silence before Cruz said, "Do you have any idea what you've got there?"

"I guess not."

"Carter, we've been looking for a link to these guys for a couple of years, but they're just about as elusive as they come. *La Tana del Lupo*—Italian for "The Den of the Wolf." Used to be part of Los Lobos, but the leader decided he was too good to stay with the gang and formed his own, even though he insists the torch was passed to him by the old leader. Raunchy Italian from Hoboken, believe it or not, who managed to weasel his way into a Texas gang. Took a bunch of guys with him. Shot up a clubhouse in Dallas and killed a bunch of Los Lobos members. They've been looking for him and his crew. We've been looking for them. Where they are, bloodshed is right around the corner. You, my friend, are sitting on a hotbed of illegal activity down there. We've gotten a few reports of this stuff going on, but never anything this organized with this many people involved." There was silence for a few seconds before Carter heard Cruz mutter, "A college campus. College kids. Those bastards. We need to stop them. And now they're directly responsible for the death of a Kentucky State Police trooper. Why am I not surprised?"

Carter was stunned. This was bigger than he'd ever dreamed. Sam was wrong—he *had* to involve KSP and KDCI with this. It was too big for his office to handle alone, that was for sure. "What do you …"

"Let me talk to my superiors, but I'm betting they'll want me to come there for a few days and work with you, get you up to speed, get all the other agencies on board. This is big, Carter. I can't tell you everything over the phone. I'll have to do it in person."

"Okay. While you're here, you're welcome to stay with me. I mean, I know the department would put you up in a hotel, but if you'd rather …"

"You know what? I'd love to stay with you. It would be nice to be with a fellow officer in a home rather than a damn hotel room. Hate to stay in the things unless I'm on vacation. And for the record, I don't snore, although there's a woman here who'd argue otherwise."

In the background, Carter heard a female voice say, "Don't let him lie to you. *Texas Chainsaw Massacre* all over again." Carter started to laugh.

"That's Mickie. Expect her to hate you if I'm coming to help you. Anything or anyone who takes me away from her even for a night is the enemy."

"Gotcha. I'll send bourbon back with you. Surely that'll placate her," Carter said, still laughing.

"Oh, I don't know about her, but it'll placate me! I'll give you a call when the arrangements are made. In the meantime, that family? The family of the girl who was involved in the shooting?"

"Yeah?"

"You need to keep an eye on them. They could be in harm's way."

Carter's stomach sank into his shoes. Well, shit. Get a break on a big case and find out the woman he was interested in could be more deeply affected by it than he'd like. "Thanks. I'll give the mother a call as soon as we hang up."

"Good deal. Talk to you soon, Carter, and thanks for calling."

"You're welcome. Thank you." Carter really wanted to say, *Wish I'd never called you*, just as the phone went dead, but that wasn't true. If his information could keep Sharla and the kids safe, he was glad to have it.

The phone only rang once on his end before he heard her say, "Hey there!"

"Hi. Got a minute?"

"For you? All the minutes you need. What's up?"

"I need to come over and talk to you."

"Now?"

"No time like the present. This can't wait."

"Well, sure. Not a problem. Come on. Have you eaten?"

Did a frozen dinner count? Carter didn't think so. "No. I haven't."

"By the time you get here, I'll have something ready."

"Okay. Thanks. And make sure your doors are locked."

A snicker came from the phone. "My doors are *always* locked. I'm a woman who lives alone."

"And your car doors?"

"Yes, Carter. My car doors too. I keep it locked up. What's going on?"

"I'll explain when I get there. Be there in a few. Bye, babe."

"Bye."

He'd called her babe. Had that been okay? Oh, who the fuck cared? He was terrified something horrible was going to happen to her, so one word wouldn't make that much difference. As he threw things together to leave, he thought about his Glock. Damn thing still wasn't back from the manufacturer, and that meant he had no handgun to give her if she didn't have one. He was using his Ruger and no way would he hand over his 1911. It was just too big and heavy for her. If she didn't have one, he'd have to get one for her and make sure she knew how to use it.

He didn't even have to knock—it appeared she'd been watching for him. "Hey there," she whispered when he stepped inside. Without giving it a second thought, he closed the door, then wrapped his arms around her waist and gave her a sweet, warm kiss. As soon as he pulled back, she smiled up at him. "I'm so glad you're here."

"I'm glad to be here," he replied and dropped a kiss on her forehead. "Something smells good."

"I hope it tastes good. Come on. Eat and tell me what's so urgent." He followed her to the kitchen and watched that glorious ass do its thing. There was a stirring below his belt, and he told the beast to quiet down.

"Oh, wow, this is good," he said as he took his first bite.

"Thanks."

How to jump in? *Oh, just go ahead and tell her*, Carter told himself. "Sharla, there's something I've got to tell you, and if you think I'm trying to scare you, then you'd be right. I found out some things today that may very well affect you, and you need to know about them."

Her brow fell. "Sounds serious."

"It is." Carter started in and watched her face closely. There was no panic there, but she was most definitely shaken. When he finished, he added, "And now I'm really concerned if you believe someone was following you."

"I've given it a lot of thought, and I'm sure of it. But why? What would anybody want with me? How deep into this was Tamara?"

"I have no idea. I'm not even sure what they're trying to do with the college kids, unless it's to use them to move drugs and guns. Otherwise, there's no use for them, no reason to involve them. Can you think of *anything* Tamara had been involved in or done in the last few months that would make you wonder what she was up to?"

Sharla shook her head. "No. Nothing. And you think this has to do with a gang in Texas?"

"A break-off from a gang in Texas. I'd say loose cannons." Carter reached across the small dining table and took Sharla's hand. "Do you have some form of protection here? A gun? Mace? Pepper spray?"

"I've got an old gun. I don't know much about it, and I've never used it. It was my dad's." Sharla squeezed Carter's hand. "I'd be lying if I said I wasn't scared at least a little."

"And you should be, but I'm going to do everything I can to find out what's going on and make sure you and the kids are safe. I'll look at the gun, figure out if it's okay, take you to the range to practice. You need to be prepared to protect yourself if necessary."

"What about the kids?"

"I have no idea what to do about them, but I'll figure it out." Carter's mind was going in a million directions, but his primary thought was to keep them safe, although he had no idea how to do that with two kids on a college campus, a place he didn't think was particularly safe to start with. "I've got an FBI guy coming up from Texas to help me sift through information and see what we can find." Well, at least Cruz thought he'd get to come. Carter hoped he hadn't just lied to Sharla. "For now, just be super vigilant."

"I will. God, Carter, this is a mess. I can't believe this. Until just a few days ago, we had normal lives, a good family … What's going to happen to us?"

"You're going to be fine, and we'll get through this."

"You said 'we'll get through this.' Are you …" She stopped and tipped her head, her eyes questioning.

"Yes. I plan to be here. I'm not going anywhere. Do you want this, us, to move forward?" Sharla nodded. "Then I think we need to be honest with the kids, not just for their safety, but so they know they have someone else they can trust. I'm sure they feel like the rug's been pulled out from under them."

"They do. Chelsea told me on Sunday that she was so sad she couldn't think. We need help, Carter. We need somebody who can guide us through this." A big silvery tear dripped down her cheek, and Carter swiped it away with his thumb.

"I'll be here." Taking her face in his hands, he tipped her head forward and kissed her on the forehead. "I care about you, Sharla, more than you know."

"I, um, have feelings for you too." Her gaze found his and Carter could see all the longing there, the loneliness and the weariness, and he suddenly found himself wanting to make it all disappear for her, to fix everything that had ever gone wrong and give her a good life. "Thank you."

That surprised him a little. "For what?"

"For being the only man who's ever been honest with me."

He shrugged. "I don't know how to be anything else."

"Yeah, but you could've blamed what happened to Tamara on one of the other officers, and yet you were honest with me about your bullet being ... Well, you know. About everything."

"I'll always be honest with you unless there's a really good reason, like something I'm not supposed to talk to you about. And if that's the case, I'll tell you that too." Without another word, he took her hand and kissed the back of it.

Sharla rose from the table, stepped to his side, and sat down on his lap. Something about that simple action made Carter feel ten feet tall. He realized in that instant Sharla was delivering herself into his hands, and he was responsible for being a man she could count on and look up to.

Carter Melton was up to the challenge. Everything he'd ever done in his life, all the struggles and disappointments and victories, they'd all led him to that moment, and he vowed to himself that he'd die before he'd screw up the relationship he was building with her. As his arms wrapped around her and pulled her tight against him, she sighed and snuggled in closer. "Carter?"

"Um-hmmm," he murmured into her hair.

"The funeral is Wednesday afternoon. Is that going to be doable for you?"

"If it's not, I'll move things around until it is. I told you I'd be there, and I'll be there for you, Chelsea, and Lionel. Whatever it takes, honey."

"Thank you. Can you stay tonight?"

"I'll have to get up super early tomorrow morning to get back home and get to work. Are you sure you want that?"

Her voice broke when she answered, "I don't want to be alone."

"Then I'm staying. I keep a few things in my car in case I have to stay with my mother overnight, so I'm good."

"You stay with your mother sometimes?"

Carter nodded. "Yeah. She fell a while back and she's been through a lot. Sometimes, if she's having a hard time or needs some help, I stay over and do things for her. Not often, but after she gave me such a scare with her last fall, if I go to see her and I can tell she's having a little trouble, I just stay."

"Awwww." Sharla stared up into his face and grinned. "Mama's boy."

"Yeah, well, if I'd fixed her banister when I should've, she wouldn't have fallen."

"So you blame yourself."

"Of course I blame myself. My dad's been gone for a

few years now. It's my responsibility to help her out, and I knew that rail was broken."

"But you're busy."

"I shouldn't be too busy to take care of people I care about. And that, my dear, is a lesson I've taken to heart."

"Guess that's good for me, huh?" she said and gave a little giggle.

"Yes, it is. Now, what time do you have to be in bed in order to get up and go to work?"

"I usually hit the hay about ten." Her hand slid down his chest and rested on his belt buckle. "But I guess we could hit it earlier."

"Nope. No sex tonight. Just sleep. And cuddling. Lots of cuddling." Carter ran his fingers through that dark hair and smiled. Regardless of the fact that she'd been the one to bring up having sex that night, he'd been the one to bring her news that set her on edge, and having sex with her would feel like he was taking advantage of her. He wasn't doing that. And the idea of her snuggled against him all night warmed him all over. "Anything you need to get done?"

"I was finishing up laundry when you called. Could you help me fold it and put it all away?"

"Of course. Tell me what you want me to do and I'll do it."

Ten minutes later, Carter found himself turning socks and folding panties. Some were Sharla's and some were obviously Chelsea's, and for reasons he didn't understand, that didn't seem weird to him at all.

It seemed … comforting. He was doing domestic things with a woman who made him *want* to do domestic things with her. He *wanted* to help her clean up the dinner dishes. He *wanted* to help her finish up the laundry. He just wanted to be with her.

At ten before ten, his hand slapped her ass playfully and she laughed aloud. "Time to get ready for bed. You need your rest," he said, grinning.

"Yes, officer!" she answered, giving him a fake salute.

"I'm going out to get my bag. Be back in a second." He watched as she retreated into the bathroom before he headed out the front door. It wasn't far to his car, maybe twenty-five feet, and Carter popped the trunk and pulled the duffel out.

As soon as the lid closed, it hit him—the sensation that he was being watched. Knowing where a pair of eyes might be was nearly impossible, but he certainly didn't want them to know he could feel them out there. Moving slowly, Carter headed back to the house, listening closely to the sounds around him. He'd almost decided he'd imagined it when he heard it.

There was a distinct rustling in the bushes across the street, faint but noticeable to his trained ear, and there wasn't a breeze. He hadn't imagined it. There really was someone out there watching him.

But they weren't. They were watching the house, of that he was sure. No way was he planning to tell Sharla. He'd just keep an eye out, and in the morning when he got up, he'd go straight to the

Hopkinsville Police Department and tell them what he suspected. He hoped like hell they'd help him keep an eye on her.

He was the sheriff of Trigg County. He didn't want to move to Christian County, but he would if he had to.

CHAPTER 5

CARTER FELT BETTER, but only a little. When Sharla got up to go to work, he left too, and he sat in his car and kept watch until she pulled out of the drive, but still no sign of anything or anyone amiss.

Instead of Hopkinsville Police, he went to the Christian County Sheriff's Department. Sheriff Glen Dowd was an old friend of his, and Carter figured if there was a way to get some eyes on Sharla, Glen would be his best bet. He wasn't wrong either—Glen had promised him not only to send a guy by while she was home, but to also talk to the police chief in town and see if they'd help out too. Thankfully, Glen said he didn't need details and that Carter's request was enough to satisfy him. Carter made a mental note to take his friend out to dinner when the investigation was over and everything was settled.

It was around eleven when he finally made it to the office, but he didn't feel bad about it. His officers were able to run things, and he never had to worry. Sure enough, he walked in to find the coffee pot full and everyone out on patrol except Justin Watson, who'd stayed behind to man the office. "Mornin', sheriff," he called when Carter stepped through the door.

"Mornin', Watson. Anything going on?"

"Mrs. Davis called and said that man was following her again, so I called her husband. He said he'd have a talk with her."

"Alzheimer's is horrible," Carter agreed with a nod.

"Yep, it is. Byron's bringing a guy in. Caught him pulling a trailer with an engine block on it, and it looks like it's the one that was stolen from Graham's house last week." Carter's cousin, Graham Melton, had reported it stolen. He'd be glad to get it back.

"Good. Anything else?"

"Uh, yeah. You got a call from some FBI guy. Livingston?"

"Yeah. Cruz Livingston. He's going to help out with the investigation into Palmer's death."

"Sweet! Didn't know you had big guns coming in! Said he'll be here Wednesday afternoon."

Well, shit. That's when the funeral is, Carter groused internally. He'd forgotten that someone had tried to call while he was talking to Glen. If he had to, he could get one of the other guys to pick Cruz up. There was no doubt in his mind that the agent would be flying into Nashville. There sure as hell wasn't any other way for him to get to Cadiz. "Okay. Thanks. I may need you to go pick him up. I'm going to Tamara Kent's funeral Wednesday afternoon."

"You're going to her funeral?" He could hear the disbelief in Watson's voice.

"Yes. I'm going."

"Don't you think that's—"

"None of your business, Watson. I think it's none of your business," he said, keeping his voice measured but firm.

"Yes, sir. None of my business."

"You know, deputy, if there's anything I've tried to teach all of you through the years, it's to have some compassion for the people we serve. Have you learned anything at all about that?"

"Yes, sir. I have. And I try to. Have compassion for them, that is. Like Mrs. Davis."

Well, now I feel like shit, Carter's brain scolded. "Yes. You do. I'm sorry, Justin. It's just that this whole thing is really eating away at me, and I know I'm distracted and acting a little weird, but I—"

"Don't worry about it. Really. You know I respect your decision to do this. If you feel you need to be there, that's your business. I couldn't do it, but I'm half the man you are."

Carter almost choked. Sometimes he forgot that the younger officers looked up to him. He thought of them as coworkers, but they thought of him as their leader. They were true professionals, and that designation, leader of their team, was a big ticket to fill. He was grateful for them, for their loyalty and hard work, and he neglected to tell them often enough. "I'm just a guy trying to do a job, Justin, but thank you. I respect all of you, and I'm sorry I don't tell you often enough. Thanks for holding down the fort this morning. Is there anything you know of that I need to address?"

"I … think Judge Michaels is coming over here."

"Oh, shit. About Edwards?" Watson nodded. "Fuck it all. Okay. Thanks for warning me. If I were you, I'd make myself scarce before he gets here."

"Roger that, sheriff. I'm gone. Think I'll patrol out in the south end of the county today. Nobody else is out there."

"Sounds good. Be safe out there," he warned Justin as the younger man strode out the door. He was thankful the worst thing that had ever happened to one of his deputies was being injured in a crash, and even then it wasn't severe. Thinking about how the KSP troopers had felt when they heard about Palmer was downright painful.

He spent the next thirty minutes arguing with Judge Michaels, who insisted he fire Edwards. He argued against it, but the judge made a compelling argument, and Carter knew it would help him straighten out the rookie deputy. Edwards wasn't bad, just sloppy, and there was no room for sloppy in their department. Zero.

As soon as Graham came with the paperwork to prove the engine block they'd seized was his, Carter got busy. There was something he wanted to check out, and it might be something Livingston could help with when he arrived. He shot a quick text to Sharla: *Tamara's dad's robbery. Where and when?*

He'd almost decided she couldn't answer because of work when his phone pinged: *O'Fallon, MO. Ten years ago in June.*

Thx. Exactly what he needed. He searched the web for the name of the local newspaper. "This is Sheriff Carter Melton from Trigg County, Kentucky. Who do I need to speak to for copies of archived papers?"

"Hold on one moment and I'll connect you."

"Thanks." Carter sat through what had to be the worst hold music rendition of Pink Floyd's "The Wall" he hoped to never hear again.

"Archives," a voice said, and he said a silent prayer of thanks that the horrible music was gone. After he'd told the woman who he was and what he wanted, he was grateful to hear her say, "Everything's on our computer now, and it's all keyword referenced. We give out complimentary subscriptions to members of the media and law enforcement. Let me set you up an account."

Five minutes and much thanks later, Carter sat in front of his computer, reading about the robbery. It really *was* botched, almost too badly screwed up to be accidental. He read every article, from the account of the robbery itself, to the clearing of the officer who'd shot Taliq Kent, and on into the arrests, trials, and sentencing of the two men who'd been with him, Brandon Estevez and Sean McCutchen. That gave him their names, and that was precisely what he was looking for.

One check on the Bureau of Prison's website found them both housed at the federal high security prison in Pennington Gap, Virginia. That was a six-hour drive unless he could find somebody who'd fly him, but he definitely wanted to talk to those two. For reasons he couldn't name, he wanted to know more about Tamara's parents. Sharla could fill him in on Imogen, but she seemed to know little about Taliq. The couple had lived outside St. Louis when he died, but that was no guarantee his family was from there, and Carter wanted to know more about them too. Any information, no matter how seemingly insignificant, could help—any.

After all, you'd never know if a rock was hiding a diamond unless you turned it over, and Carter was all about turning over stones.

* * *

"Put on something nice. Not dressy, just casual, but nice."

"Why?"

"You ask too many questions!" Carter said and laughed.

"Oh, I do, do I? Okay. Casual dress it is. When?"

"About five thirty?"

"Um, okay. See you then."

"Yep. I'll be there." Carter hit END and sat there, wondering what she'd say when she figured out what he was doing.

He swapped his cruiser out for his pickup truck and

dressed in slacks and a button-front shirt, a nice blue plaid that he'd gotten on sale at the mall area in Paducah. To his delight, he passed a Christian County Sheriff's Department cruiser on his way into Sharla's neighborhood, and he was pretty sure they were checking the house. Good. Glen was holding true to his promise. He'd barely gotten the truck parked when he looked up and saw her standing there in the open doorway, leaning up against the jamb and smiling with her arms folded across her chest, and he couldn't help but smile back. God, she was beautiful! As soon as he stepped out and closed the truck door, he heard her say, "You're certainly a punctual kinda guy, Carter Melton."

"I am. Makes it easier when I've got something to look forward to."

"You're awfully dressed up."

Carter looked down at himself. "Yeah? I guess I clean up okay."

"You clean up more than okay. Come here." The door barely closed behind him before she leaned in and kissed him—hard.

He was laughing when he pulled back. "Whew! That's a helluva greeting!"

"You're a helluva guy! So what's this big secret?"

"Ready to go?"

"Would help if I knew where I was going," she answered, hands on her hips.

"Trust me?"

He knew that was a loaded question, and he

grinned when she said, "Absolutely. Okay. You want to surprise me, I'll let you. Let's go."

They chatted as he drove along, her about some of the patients she'd had that day—no names, of course—and him about Judge Michaels' visit. Boy, he dreaded the conversation he'd be having with Edwards, but now it wasn't coming just from him. It was coming from the judge too, so it would carry a lot more weight. They'd driven more than twenty-five miles from the interstate exit when Sharla said with a grin, "We're going to Paducah!"

"Nope. We're not. You'll be surprised, I promise." Glancing at her there in the truck, his chest warmed at the smile on her lips as she watched out the truck window. She was excited, and that was exactly what he wanted.

He got off at the Calvert City exit and headed east until he came to the spur that sent him over to the state park. "Oh! I've never been here!" Sharla exclaimed as he turned into the drive.

"The food is really good. I've been here several times. They actually have a buffalo dinner here once a year." Carter wheeled into a parking spot in the oval parking lot and shut the truck off. "I always enjoyed that."

"I probably would too. I like to try things I've never had before, and I don't think I've ever had buffalo. Can we come back for that?"

"Sure. It's after the first of the year, so it'll be a while." *Will she still be interested in me after the first of the year?* he wondered. There was no doubt in his mind that he'd still be interested in her.

The dining room was almost deserted. Most of their business came in the summer, being a state resort park, and that was one reason he'd chosen it. "Could you seat us by the window?" he asked as the hostess greeted them.

"Sure! Right this way." Pointing to a table in the back corner at the huge plate glass window, the server left them and Carter helped Sharla into her chair. It was great to be able to sit there and look out over the enormous man-made Kentucky Lake, and they had a good view of the pedestrian bridge, the breakwater jetty, and the marina. Carter had never been interested in having a boat, but it sure looked inviting down there.

They talked and laughed through dinner. She ordered a Kentucky hot brown, which she declared delicious, and he ordered a steak with a baked potato. Their salad bar was fresh and plentiful, and before long both diners were stuffed. "Whew! I'm tight as a tick!"

Sharla laughed. "Me too. I think I need to walk some of this off. Could we ..."

"Sure can. Let me take care of the check and we'll go out and walk around a bit."

The early fall air was warm, but when they headed down the hill and toward the shoreline, a cool breeze wafted up from the water. Sharla reached for his hand and smiled. "This is really nice."

Carter took hers and squeezed it. "It is. Very nice.

The company's better than the food and the scenery though." She didn't get a chance to speak before he drew her hand upward and kissed the back of it.

She stopped dead, their hands still clasped. "Can this really go anywhere, Carter? I don't want to be played with."

"This morning, when my deputy found out I was going to the funeral and he questioned my judgment, I told him it was none of his business. And it's not. As long as I don't compromise the investigation in any way, it's nobody's concern. Do I think it would be best to keep it on the down low? Yeah, until it's all over. If somebody finds out, am I going to be ruined? Nope. We don't need to flaunt it, but I'm not going to run away from it forever. We're building something here, Sharla, something good, and I don't want to mess that up because I'm afraid of what other people think."

"I feel the same way. People can think what they want. Besides, there's probably nothing to any of this, just a huge mistake on Tam's part."

Should he tell her? He didn't want to tell her everything. After all, they might discover there wasn't much to it. But he also didn't want to keep anything from her. Even so, with the funeral coming up, she didn't need anything else to worry about. He decided to go straight up the middle of that road. "Actually, there may be more. We don't know yet."

Her brow furrowed immediately. "What do you mean?"

"Not sure yet. We're following some leads. Nothing to worry about, though."

She gave him a suspicious side-eye with one brow raised. "Between the time I got home and you got there, I saw two cop cars pass my house, a city and a county. Do you know anything about that?"

Not gonna lie to her, he told himself. "I might."

Turning loose of his hand abruptly, she gaped and her eyes popped open wide. "Am I some kind of suspect?"

"God, no!" he almost shrieked. "Of course not! If you were suspected of something, I most certainly wouldn't be here! Good lord, woman, what in hell would you be suspected of? Why? Have you done something you shouldn't have?"

"Yeah. I slept with the sheriff of Trigg County," she said and gave a nervous little laugh.

"Oh, very funny. No. Last time I checked that didn't break a Kentucky Revised Statute. But I did ask my friend Glen if he could—"

"Glen? The sheriff, Glen?"

"Yes. We all *do* talk to each other, you know."

"And what did you tell him?"

"I didn't. And, to his credit, he didn't ask. I think he felt like that was on a need-to-know basis and if it was me asking, that was good enough and he didn't need to know." She had no idea how thankful he was for that little extension of professional courtesy.

"Oh. Okay then. You really think that's necessary?"

"I do, especially since you think somebody's been

watching you." No way would he tell her about the rustling in the bushes. Nope. That was just another thing she didn't need to hear about.

"So you believe me?"

"Of *course* I believe you. Why wouldn't I?" He wanted to add, *Because I heard them*, but he didn't. "If you think you're being watched, then you're being watched, and I'm going to do whatever I can to keep you safe."

"Thank you." She stood in silence for a minute as though she wanted to say something and didn't know how. Carter was about to speak when she said, "You told me you hadn't been with anybody in a couple of years. Were you in a relationship?"

He'd known it was going to come up some time. "Actually, I was. Her name is Mandy, and we were together for about five years."

"But you weren't married?"

"Nope. Wasn't me. I wanted to get married, but she didn't, not unless I found a different job. And that wasn't going to happen." *Might as well broach the subject*, he thought. "Most women don't want to be involved with law enforcement officers. They worry, they're afraid, they're alone a lot of the time because our jobs aren't nine to five. We have a lot to deal with—murders, assaults, rapes, child abuse, high-speed chases, people shooting at us, trying to stab us, drug addicts OD-ing in our cars, you name it—and it can seep into our relationships. In the end, she just couldn't take it. There came a tipping point, and she was gone."

Her eyes were sad when she asked, "What was the tipping point?"

"We had a big drug bust and in the process, I was grazed. Nothing serious, just a flesh wound, but it totally freaked her out. She said she couldn't take wondering if the next phone call she got would be from the coroner. I told her that could happen with anything—car accident, heart attack, stroke—but she said the chances were so much greater for me that she wasn't willing to live like that anymore. She moved out and I haven't spoken to her since."

"Wow."

"Yeah. Five years down the drain." He sat for a minute, wondering if he should ask the twenty-million-dollar question, and decided the time was right. After all, she'd brought it up. "So I have to ask ... Could you live that way? Knowing every time someone you loved left the house, they could be stabbed or shot?"

Her voice was soft and a tear rolled down her cheek. "After what's happened with Tam, I think I could live through just about anything."

"Doesn't matter. This is different. It's the constant threat. Long nights. Long days. Weekends. Holidays. Not everyone would want to deal with all that. You need to think about that. You need to be sure before this goes any farther."

A sound came from her throat, a tiny choking sound, as she reached for his hand and clutched it. Another tear rolled down her cheek, but her eyes were clear. "I'm sure. Carter, I'm falling for you, and if you don't feel the same way, you need to tell me. Please. I've had so much heartache and disappointment in my life. I don't need more."

It wasn't how he'd pictured it, but with the air moving across the surface of the water and the light fading, Carter had one simple, shining moment, and he had to make it count. "Honestly, I think I fell in love with you the first second I saw you."

There wasn't a chance to say another word. Sharla stepped up to him and kissed him, her arms locking around his neck almost as though he were saving her from drowning. Clutching her to him, Carter could feel it all around them, the magic of love newly found, of broken hearts mending and tired ones starting over. When she broke the kiss, she gave him a smile that he'd remember on his deathbed. "I love you, Carter. No man has ever done to me what you do or given me as much of himself as you have. I know it's fast, but I don't care. If you disappeared from my life tomorrow, nothing would ever be the same."

He chucked her under the chin and whispered to her, "I'm not going anywhere, little girl. I'm here to stay. It's a shame that it took a tragedy for us to find each other, but we have, and I won't apologize for that, not now, not ever." The kiss he gave her was sweet and warm, and his tongue teased the seam of her lips until she parted them slightly. When he deepened it, she opened to him as her tongue explored his. They stood like that for a time they'd never have again, the first kiss of confessed love, and Carter hoped that kiss would go on forever. He'd given up, and just when he'd thought it was hopeless, he'd found her, the woman he'd always wanted. As the kiss cooled, they both leaned in, their foreheads touching, and he heard her sigh. "Sharla, we're going to get through this. I promise. And we're going to come out the other side and have a good life."

"You sound so sure of that."

"I am. Come on. Let's go home." Taking her hand, he led her back up the hill, walking together in silence until they reached the truck. Once he'd helped her in, he patted her hands as they lay in her lap. "The kids will be home tomorrow night because of the funeral on Wednesday. Want to come to my house tonight?"

The nod she gave him was almost childlike. "I'd like that."

"Okay. Let's stop somewhere and pick up something we can have for breakfast. You'll have to get up early tomorrow to get to work."

"Doesn't matter as long as I get to be there with you tonight." Her fingers stroked down his cheek and he felt that little quickening in his chest, the one that told him it was really happening. A woman was giving him her heart. He couldn't break it, bruise it, or drop it. He'd be the man who kept it safe. He *had* to be.

They picked up a package of cream cheese Danishes, the coffee she liked, and some half and half for it. Before they left, he pointed to the health and beauty section. "Go get yourself a toothbrush and whatever toothpaste you like."

"If you're sure …"

"I'm positive," he said with a smile and watched her head off that direction. That was the moment it hit him. *I've got a girlfriend!* It was all he could do to keep from bursting out laughing. Wouldn't his mom be surprised?

As soon as they walked through the door, he headed to the bedroom. "I'm going to find you a big tee shirt to wear. I know I've got a few." As he prowled through the dresser drawer where he kept them, he heard her call out something. "I'm sorry, what did you say?"

"I said, is this you and your parents?"

He knew what she was looking at and grinned to himself. "Yeah. That's us."

The incredulity in her voice was loud and clear when she asked, "You and your parents went *skydiving?*"

"Yeah. My dad was dying with cancer. You know that song, "Live Like You Were Dying?"

"Yeah?"

"Well, he took that to heart. He had this whole list of things he wanted to do, and that was one of them. There was also mountain climbing—"

"And did you—"

"Yep. Black Mountain. Tallest peak in Kentucky. Then there was deep sea fishing. We did that off the coast of Florida. He wanted to live through a Maine winter. I didn't get to go for that—I had to work, of course—but he and Mom rented a little house up there and stayed the winter. She made it clear they'd never be doing *that* again!" Carter laughed as he remembered his mother telling him about the day they couldn't open the door until a neighbor came to their rescue with a snow blower. He stepped into the living room with a dark green tee shirt in his hand and held it out to her. "And he wanted to go gambling, so we went to Las Vegas and he blew five thousand dollars."

She took the tee and turned for him to unzip her dress. "Five thousand? Good grief!"

"Yeah. My mom sure could've used that money later, but she wanted him to be able to check if off his bucket list so she'd have no regrets." The skin revealed under the zipper made his palms itch with desire, and he didn't even ask, just unsnapped her bra while he was at it.

It didn't seem to faze her in the least as she dropped the dress and the bra and pulled the tee over her head. "Why didn't you just go to one of the casino boats closer?"

Carter snickered. "Because he also wanted to see the showgirls."

"Ah. Dirty old man," Sharla said and winked.

"Yep. Guess the apple doesn't fall too far from the tree, huh?" He reached for her waist with both hands but before he could grip it, she grabbed his shirt, untucked it from his pants, and languorously began to unbutton it. "I'm glad you can't read my mind right now. Or maybe I wish you could," he whispered as he watched her fingers work the buttons loose.

She gave him a wicked grin. "Oh, I can read your mind. I know what you want, and I want it too, so I guess that makes me a dirty old man just like you, huh?" Pushing his shirt open, she lifted it up and back over his shoulders and he let it fall to the floor. Her fingers trailed up his abs and through the hair on his chest until they came to rest on his collarbone. "You have to be the sexiest guy I've ever met, Carter."

A chuckle rumbled from his throat. "Don't get out much, do you?"

"Just say thank you, baby," she whispered and kissed the side of his neck. His already-primed manhood sprang upward in an instant.

His voice was more of a groan when he whispered back, "Thank you, baby."

"You're welcome. Come on." Taking his hand, she led him to the bedroom. They were almost through the door when he broke away, ran into the living room, turned off the lamp, and jetted back into the bedroom with her.

"Now where were we?" he asked, wrapping his arms around her waist and pulling her toward the bed. When the back of his knees hit the edge, he let himself fall backward onto its soft surface, taking her with him.

"I think you were about to tell me how much you love me," she whispered and kissed his chin.

"Ah, yes. That was it. And I do, Sharla. I love you and I want to show you how much I love you."

"And I love you and want to show you how much I love you." She kissed his chin again, then down his neck, down his chest, down his abs, and Carter almost prayed aloud that he was right about what was coming next.

It only took her a few seconds to undo his belt and unbutton and unzip his slacks, and when she gave them and his boxer briefs a hard tug, every inch of his manhood shot straight up to greet her. She licked up his length once, twice, three times, and then teased the head with her lips. "Oh, Jesus, girl, you're killin' me."

"I'm just getting started." Her tongue teased his slit for a few seconds before she opened wide and took almost his whole length in. Carter let out a moan that he was sure made the curtains flutter as Sharla sucked him hard and moved up and down his shaft. Wet. Hot. Tight. God, he needed that, needed her, and his hands wound into her hair, not tightly, but more like a sweet caress. He let out a little chuckle as she worked until she let loose with a *pop*. "What's so funny?"

"You said you're just getting started, but I won't last long at this rate," he said, starting to laugh in earnest.

"Well, then, let's get it going, shall we?" she said, laughing along with him, and went back to sucking him with even greater gusto.

Carter was in heaven. No matter what happened, as long as he knew she was hanging on, he'd be okay. They had to get to the other side of all the mess that had brought them together and they'd be fine. When she wrapped her hand around his cock and pumped as she sucked, he wanted to die from sheer happiness. In seconds, he felt it, that point of no return, and his balls emptied into her throat. "Oh my god. That was … Oh my god. You're good at that, girl."

Still licking him clean, she stopped and grinned up at him. "Thanks."

"Get up here with me." As soon as she scooted up the bed, Carter sucked a nipple into his mouth and let his hand roam downward until it found that sweet little rocket launcher that could make her lift off. She writhed against him, her lips on his, as he drove her upward, and when her hand found him at half mast, it didn't take her long to get him hard again. He devoured her, every inch of her he could reach, and he considered burying his face between her thighs, but he wanted to kiss her and look into her eyes as he made her come.

Sucking his lower lip until she could nip it, she turned loose and gasped. "Oh, god, Carter, make me come. I need it. I need it so bad, baby. Please?"

"Oh, you will, precious," he whispered against her skin and watched her nipples peak twice as hard as they were seconds before. Rolling them to their sides, he slipped inside her and kept stroking her tiny pearl, listening to her cry out and feeling her twitch against him. She was growing more frantic and he gave her two little strokes of his cock, just enough to rub her G-spot and tip her over the edge. Her belly clenched, her hands gripped him, and her hips thrusted against him until he stopped and flipped her onto her back, rising above her, his hardness still buried inside her. Two hard, driving strokes pierced her when he whispered to her, "I love you, Sharla. I'm not letting this go."

Her voice was raspy and breathless as she whispered, "Oh, Carter. Yeah. Please, fuck me, babe. Just like that."

"I'm not fucking you, baby. We're making love. I want you to know what this is, what it means to me, what I hope it means to you."

"It does, Carter, I promise. I want to be with you forever. Please, please, never leave me," she pleaded as he pounded inside her.

"I told you, I'm not going anywhere. You're stuck with me. Look down, Shar. Look at where we're joined. It's beautiful, babe." Carter glanced down and watched his shaft disappearing into her body, into that warm, wet haven that had breathed life back into his heart. "You're the most beautiful thing I've ever laid eyes on, babe. I've never wanted any woman the way I want you."

"I've never wanted a man the way I want you. You're everything to me, Carter. You're, you're, oh, god, I'm … yeah," she said with a moan as the orgasm took her.

Carter was right behind her, and that time when he emptied himself into her, it felt sacred and holy, like a sacrament. They were one, he and this beautiful woman. She was his. He was hers. She made him complete.

They lay together in the dark bedroom, panting and

clutching each other. His lips found hers and he gave her a soft kiss before moving to kiss her forehead. "Sleep, babe. Morning comes early."

Her voice was drowsy and small. "Okay. I love you, Carter."

"I love you too, baby." Pulling her close, he smiled as her cheek rested against his pec and her warmth enveloped him. He loved her and he was loved. What else could he ask for?

To solve the mystery of what happened to Tamara. And then they'd be free.

* * *

WATCHING HER IN THE MORNING LIGHT FROM THE kitchen's small window would become his favorite new pastime, he decided. Her hair was a mess and she was wearing his old tee shirt, but she was still the most beautiful thing he'd ever seen. As soon as she took the last bite of her Danish, she sighed. "Guess I'd better go get dressed."

"Yeah. I've got to drive you to Hoptown to do the walk of shame from my car to the house. You gonna be able to handle that?" he asked with a grin.

"Oh, yeah. I think I will, although I have to say, walking is going to be a little difficult." He watched with amusement as she stood and winced.

He let out a snort. "What's wrong? Can't handle the big guy?"

"Looked like I handled him pretty well last night."

She kissed the top of his head as she passed him on her way to the bedroom. "At least it sure seemed that way."

"Yeah, you did a good job, and I'm hard to please, so that's really saying something for you." He was grinning when she turned and shot him the bird. "Don't be like that!" he called out, laughing.

"You taking me home in nothing but your underwear?" she called out from the bedroom, so Carter got up and headed that way to dress. He'd already decided he'd just put on his clothes from the night before, take her home, and come back to shower. It was damn early and he had plenty of time.

They rolled up in front of her house and Carter stopped the truck. "Want me to walk you up?"

"Yes, please." Something in her voice told him she was anxious, and he wasn't sure why. Had she seen something? Or someone? Didn't matter. He'd gladly walk her to the door.

When it was unlocked and she stepped inside, she turned to him. "We won't get to be together tonight, but I'll call you when the kids get settled, okay?"

"Sure. Sounds good. Be thinking about when we want to tell them about us, because we're going to have to."

She nodded. "I know. I think we should wait about a week, don't you?"

"Maybe. Let's see how tomorrow goes."

"Okay." Taking his face in her hands, she kissed him lightly and gave him a tender smile. "I love you, Carter."

"I love you too. Talk to you later. Bye, babe." The

door clicked closed as he made his way down the steps and when he got to his truck and slipped inside, he looked back. Her face appeared in the window and she gave him a little wave before disappearing behind the sheer curtains.

The drive back home was uneventful, but the morning would have its own excitement. He had a rather unpleasant task ahead of him, and he was thankful the coffee pot was full when he reached the office. Durst looked up from his desk and gave a nod, and Carter scanned the room until he found the other deputy. "Edwards, I need to speak to you, please. In my office."

"Coming, sheriff," the younger man answered and Carter could hear his footfalls as he stepped through the doorway. "Close the door," he said without even turning around, and he heard it shut quietly. "Have a seat."

He turned to find Edwards sitting in the chair in front of his desk, both feet on the floor and hands on his knees. There was no doubt he was nervous, as well he should be. "Do you know why you're in here?"

"No, sir."

"I got a visit from Judge Michaels."

"Sir?"

"He's pretty damn unhappy with you wasting his time in court."

"I'm sorry, sir, I—"

"He threw out four of your tickets the other day,

Edwards. Four. Out of the ten we had in there, how many were yours?"

The rookie's face reddened. "Five, sir."

"That's eighty percent, young man. Eighty percent of your citations were thrown out. Do you know why?"

"No, sir."

"Because they weren't filled out properly. So this afternoon, I want you here in the office. I'm going to write out five scenarios for traffic stops and I want you to write tickets for them. Then we're going to go over them and figure out what it is you're not doing correctly. In the meantime, I want you to pull some of the copies from Lewis, Watson, and Durst, and compare them to what you've been doing. Then when you work on the new ones, I want you to be able to tell me what you did wrong. Got that?"

The younger man dropped his gaze to the floor in embarrassment. "Yes, sir."

"We all have to learn, Edwards, but I thought you'd been taught how to do this properly. Apparently not. And the next time Judge Michaels has to come over here and crawl up my ass, it had better be for somebody else's screw-ups, got it?"

"Yes, sir."

"Okay. Go finish your activity logs from yesterday and get them filed, and then we'll work on these."

The deputy's eyes shot up. "I'm not patrolling today?"

"No. You definitely are not. You're going to man the phones so Durst can get out there in a cruiser and do what you should be doing." He hated to do that to Durst, but the seasoned deputy was eight weeks post-operative for his knee injury and he'd been cleared for full duty, so it was time for him to get back out there anyway.

"Yes, sir. I'm sorry, sir."

"Sorry is a bad word to have to use in our profession, rookie. A lot of times when we have to say we're sorry, somebody's died. So let's try to not have to use it again, shall we?"

"Yes, sir. I'll get right on it, sir."

"Good. I'll get those scenarios out to you so you can start working on them." Carter pointed to the door. "Back to work."

"Yes, sir." Edwards stood and made his way out of the office. Without being told, he closed the door behind him, and Carter sighed. Personnel issues—he hated 'em.

The information on the annual sheriff's conference had shown up, and Carter took some time to look it over. It was being held that summer in Jamestown at Lake Cumberland State Resort Park. He looked forward to the conferences, but he dreaded them too. A lot of the guys brought their wives, and he always felt left out. Maybe Sharla could come with him. It would be a nice trip for her. They usually planned things for the spouses, and she could meet some of the other sheriffs' wives.

Would he like for her to be his wife? The question made him smile. In a lot of ways, that sounded good.

Of course, there was the fear factor. Would she be able to handle his profession? She said she could, and he believed her. It was a little early for rings and wedding bells, but he didn't mind fantasizing about it. Kissing her good morning every morning, coming home to her in the evenings, dinner at the table instead of on a tray in front of the TV ... wouldn't those things be nice? They sure would, he decided. Time would tell, and he'd definitely give it as much time as necessary.

Just as he was slipping the information back into the envelope, his phone buzzed and he hit the button. "Yeah?"

"Sir, it's Detective Curry from Calloway County on line one for you."

"Thanks, Edwards. I'll take it." He picked up the receiver on the office phone and hit the button. "Sam!"

"Hey, Carter! How's it goin'?"

"Goin' good! Cruz is coming in tomorrow."

"So I heard! Would it bother you too much for me to pick him up?"

"Bother me? Hell no, not at all. I was wondering how I was going to get him here and be at that funeral at the same time."

"You're going to the funeral?"

Well, shit, here we go, Carter thought. "Yeah. The family's requested that I be there."

"Well, I have to say, my respect for you just skyrocketed. Most officers wouldn't want any part of being at a funeral where they'd taken down the deceased. That's going to be awkward for you, I'm sure, but I admire you for that."

That was *not* what he'd thought Sam would say, and for that little slice of time, his heart was grateful for the understanding of the officer on the phone. "Thank you. I just want to do whatever they need me to do."

"I get it. I do. So do you know Cruz's plans?"

"No. He hasn't told me yet."

"I'll give him a call and get all the particulars," Sam offered.

"He's probably flying into Nashville. Sure you don't mind?" That wasn't Sam's responsibility, after all.

"Not at all. I'll take Dahlia with me and we'll grab something to eat on the way back, spend some time catching up. We didn't even know about Mickie until recently, so it would be good to spend some time with him."

"Okay, if you're sure. I'll be at the funeral tomorrow afternoon, so if you need anything, just send me a text. And thanks, Sam. Thanks for everything."

"You're quite welcome. Always happy to help. And good luck tomorrow, Carter. My hat's off to you."

"Thank you." They hung up and Carter sat there for a little while, contemplating everything. An FBI agent was coming to help him. To his knowledge, no one with KSP or KDCI knew that—yet. And he had no intention of telling them. Deep in thought, he barely heard the tap at the door. "Come in."

"Sheriff?"

"Yes?"

"Sir, I have every intention of doing what you want me to do, but I pulled some of Durst and Watson's tickets and, honestly, I can't see what I'm doing wrong."

Oh, for the love of god, Carter wanted to sigh out, but he couldn't. *Patience*, he told himself. "Okay. Nothing looks different?"

"No, sir. If I'm doing something wrong, I don't see it."

"Here. Give me one of both and let me look at them." Carter took them from Edwards' hands and squinted at them. He followed down the page. Everything seemed to be there—the deputy's name, date, time, location, name of citation recipient, license number, license plate number, KRS citing. The deputies had signed them at the bottom. What was missing? He couldn't see it either. He was about to say exactly that when he caught it. "Oh my fucking god."

"What, sir?"

"This little box down here. See it?" Carter pointed at the box just below the deputy's signature. Edwards leaned in and squinted at it. "You didn't check that."

"What is that, sir?"

"It says," Carter said, still squinting at the tiny print, "'I hereby certify that I am a duly-sworn officer of the law and am within my full rights to issue this citation on behalf of the Trigg County Sheriff's Department.' You have *got* to be *shitting* me. *That's* what Michaels was having such a fit over?" Carter could barely believe his eyes. "I just ... Edwards, I'm sorry. I don't know ... Had you just never noticed that before?"

"No, sir. I don't remember anybody ever mentioning it to me, and it's so tiny I couldn't even read it."

"Me neither. I always just checked it because I was told to, but if you weren't, hell, there's no way you could've known. Need a damn magnifying glass to even see it. Tell you what. I'm going to tell old Judge Michaels that you're going to the vision center and we're going to forget this ever happened, okay? I can't believe that old sumbitch … You're doing a good job, young man. Don't let this rattle you. And I'm sorry I came off so hard-assed earlier."

"It's okay, sheriff. Thanks for the help. I want to do everything right, I really do. And I know you've got a lot on your mind."

"I do. Thank you for being understanding. Now go get back to work. Go to the vision center at the super-store and look at a pair of frames so I won't be lying when I tell him you visited there."

Edwards gave Carter a lopsided grin. "Thanks, sheriff. I'll do that." Just as before, Edwards closed the door softly behind him when he left Carter's office and the sheriff slid back into his chair and sighed. Dear god. With all he had going on, Michaels was on a rampage about *that*? He shook his head in frustration. *That old man should have half my problems*, Carter thought as he went through a stack of documents on his desk.

One more day. Cruz would be there and maybe they could start unraveling the puzzle that surrounded

Tamara's death. After a call to the county court clerk's office, Carter headed over to their office to pick up a check from the department's funds, then headed to the funeral home to deliver it. Tamara's funeral was paid for. Her headstone was being paid for by a church there in the area. The grave digging and opening?

Carter paid for that himself. It was the very least he could do.

CHAPTER 6

IT HAD BEEN his habit over the years to pick up a random book, open it to a random page, and start reading. He didn't look at the cover or the spine, nor did he look at the top of the page. He didn't want to know the name of the book; he wanted to read a bit in it and try to remember the title and author.

The book that evening had dropped open to page two hundred eighty-seven and he'd read three pages when he figured out it was a John Grisham novel. Time slipped by as he thought about it and decided it was *The Client*. He'd gotten through eight pages when his phone rang and he looked at the screen. *I've got to assign her a ringtone*, he thought as he answered it. "Hey, babe."

"Hi. I think everybody's down for the night."

"They doing okay?"

"I gave them both a Benadryl before they went to bed. That'll help them sleep. Tomorrow's going to be hard. Did you have a good day?"

"Yes and no. By the way, everything's taken care of. I dropped the department fund's check off at the funeral home, and the excavation is paid for too. And according to the funeral director, Trinity Christian Church is going to pay for the headstone." When she didn't reply, Carter asked softly, "Honey, you okay?"

He could hear the sob in her voice as she answered. "I just … Thank you for taking care of all that. I don't think I could. I've been a wreck all day. You can't know how badly I'm dreading tomorrow, not just for me, but for Chelsea and Lionel. That poor boy … He feels like he's lost everything. I've tried to be a good parent to him, done my best, but—"

"You've done a fine job, sweetheart. I can't imagine how he feels, though. But at least he's got you and Chelsea."

"And you, Carter."

"Yes. And me. Even though he doesn't know it yet." He had to smile just a little at the thought. It wasn't just Chelsea he'd be taking on. Lionel would come with the package too. Yes, they were adults, but they were still Sharla's children, and he'd still want a good relationship with them both. "So how do you want tomorrow to go down?"

"Can you sit with us?"

"I can, but I'd rather be up and keeping an eye out. There's a possibility that if there's something wrong going on with all this, somebody might turn up at the service or the cemetery. I want to be able to see what's going on, and I can't if I'm sitting in a pew. Will that be okay?"

"Yeah, I guess. Just knowing you're there will make me feel better," she answered, and he could hear the sorrow in her weak voice.

"But I'll most definitely drive you to the funeral home, to the cemetery, and then back home. Oh, I meant to tell you, I got a call from one of the women in the alumni association at the school. They want to provide a meal for you guys after the service, if you'd like. Said they'd bring the food to the funeral home and you could pick it up afterward to take home. Nothing fancy, just some folks trying to do something nice for you." All he heard from the other end of the phone was a sob. "Sharla, honey, it's okay. Everybody wants to help you. Let them, okay?"

"I feel so bad for Trooper Palmer's family!" she cried out. "Who's helping them? Is anybody doing anything for them? It has to be awful!"

"Oh, yeah. The troopers have all rallied around them, and KSP takes care of everything. They've got everything they need. Don't worry about them. They'll be fine. Just worry about yourself, Chelsea, and Lionel. That's your only responsibility right now. You're not responsible for what Tamara did, babe. That's not your fault."

"I just feel so bad for them."

"I know. We all do. And we all feel bad for you too. This isn't something you would've ever chosen for your family."

"It sure as hell isn't." She was silent for a few seconds before she said, "Oh, I almost forgot. The damn TV station out of Nashville called me today, wanting an interview. I told them to go fuck themselves."

"Good move. Don't talk to them—don't talk to *anybody*. The investigation is ongoing, and it's not appropriate. Plus you really don't know anything to tell them, and anything personal about Tamara, well, they can dig around on their own. You shouldn't help them."

"That was my thinking too. Carter, I … I'm just so damn tired."

"I know, honey. Let's get through tomorrow and you can get some rest. And babe?"

"Yeah?"

"I love you."

He could hear her start to cry again. "I love you too. I'm so sorry for all of this."

"None of it is your fault, angel. Just go to bed and get some sleep. I'll be there tomorrow at eleven forty-five to pick all of you up, okay?"

"Okay. Thanks. See you then."

"You will. Bye, love." He hit END and dropped back into the sofa's softness. The next day would be hell on earth, and he hoped she could hang on.

* * *

IT WASN'T SOMETHING CARTER HAD GIVEN MUCH thought to before, but he found himself wishing the sheriff's department had a "dress" uniform that Wednesday morning. Lewis served as his detective, and he and Carter both had polo shirts with the department's crest embroidered on the breast pocket. Fortunately, that kept his regular uniform in the closet, clean, pressed, and ready, and he donned it and looked in the mirror. Plenty nice enough, he supposed, for a regular, everyday uniform.

His cruiser was more than large enough for all four of them, so he headed to Sharla's to pick up her, Chelsea, and Lionel. It was about eleven forty when he pulled into the drive, and he decided to just go ahead and ring the doorbell.

A red-eyed, teary Chelsea answered the door. "Hi, Chelsea. You guys about ready?"

"Yeah. Mom's just finishing up. Would you like to come in?"

She has no idea I've slept in her mother's bed, his brain hummed. "Sure. Thanks."

"Just have a seat. I'm sure she'll be out in a minute. I've got to go help Lionel with his tie." As Chelsea walked away, he heard her grumble, "Like I know anything about ties."

A chance to be useful and help out. Better grab it. "I'd be glad to help him."

"Oh. Well, yeah, maybe that would be better. Hey, Li, Sheriff Melton said he'd help you with your tie," Chelsea called down the hallway.

The young man appeared in what had to be a brand new suit, his eyes puffy but dry. "Okay. I don't tie these things so I don't know anything about them."

"It's not hard if you know how. This'll only take a second." Carter adjusted the length of both ends of the tie, then began the process of knotting it. When it was finished, he stepped back and looked at it. "Looks nice."

"Thanks." That one word was the only thing Lionel said before he walked on past Carter and out the front door. What he was doing out there, Carter couldn't imagine, and he couldn't tell if the young man was overcome with emotion or pissed off that he was there. A sound caused Carter to turn.

Sharla stood there in a navy dress and low black pumps, her hair caught up in a smooth chignon he was sure Chelsea had helped her arrange. "Hi. Everybody ready to go?" she asked as she strode across the room toward him. The urge to grab her and kiss her was overwhelming, but he knew he couldn't—not in front of Chelsea anyway. "Where's Lionel?"

"Outside. I think he might be mad that I'm here," Carter murmured under his breath.

Sharla shook her head. "I don't think so. He's just trying hard not to show any emotion. Thinks crying is a sign of weakness."

"Would you like for me to talk to him?"

"Only if it comes about organically. Don't force it or make a point to do it, but if he's close by and tries to interact with you, sure. Talk to him. He doesn't have a man in his life except for one teacher at the school."

Carter nodded. "Noted. You ready?"

"As ready as I'll ever be for this, I suppose. Chels?"

"Yeah. I'm ready, Mom."

"Then let's get everybody in my car and head that direction." Carter opened the door and waited for the two women to step out, then locked the knob and pulled it shut behind him. Chelsea and Lionel were already sliding into the back seat, so he opened the front passenger door for Sharla and waited until she was buckled in to close it.

The ride to the funeral home was painful. Carter could tell no one really felt like talking. Several times he glanced over at Sharla, but she was staring out the window, not looking toward him, and he couldn't catch her eye. Family visitation was at noon, and they made it there with three minutes to spare.

As soon as they pulled up in the parking lot, Carter turned to them. "I will be here partially because you all asked me to be and partially as a professional. I won't be sitting with you; I'll be standing in the back to one side, keeping an eye out. If there's a problem, I want to catch it fast."

Sharla's eyes popped open wide. "You don't really think there'll be a problem, do you?"

All Carter could do was shrug. "There are nut jobs everywhere. If one of them decides to target the funeral, I want somebody to take them down fast. I know people are upset that a trooper has been killed, but I'm hoping everyone understands that this service is for you guys, not Tamara. I talked to Sheriff Dowd and he's going to have a few guys around. But there's something else I need to talk to you about, so pay attention." When Chelsea and Lionel's eyes found his, he continued. "If you see anything, and I mean *anything*, that doesn't look right, anybody you think shouldn't be there or anybody or anything that stands out in your mind, I need you to tell somebody. One of the officers. I mean it. Don't hesitate." *Should I? Yep. I think it's time*, he told himself. "We think Tamara was intentionally drugged."

"I knew it!" Lionel shouted.

"If that's the case, the old saying that the perpetrator always comes back to the scene of the crime, well, it's not always true, but it is a lot of times. It's possible somebody might show up that would need to be talked to, and I don't want them to slip away. Got it?"

"Yes, sir. I'll keep an eye out," Chelsea assured him.

"We all will. Right, Lionel?" Sharla added.

"Yes. I will."

Carter gave them an affirmative nod. "Good. Let's go."

He hung back appropriately inside while the three of them were led into the small chapel by the funeral director. The sounds of Chelsea and Sharla crying were heart-piercing to him, and he listened carefully for Lionel's grief, but he heard nothing from the boy. They'd been in the chapel for about fifteen minutes when he heard footsteps and saw Lionel come pounding through the doors. "Lionel! Wait up!" The boy glanced back at him and rounded a corner, so Carter picked up the pace to catch up.

He caught Lionel just as the young man reached the back door. "Leave me alone!" he barked back.

"Lionel! Wait! Let's talk, okay?" They both stopped just outside the door, Lionel's back still turned to Carter. "Look, I know this is hard. It's gotta be. Losing somebody is never easy. But Chelsea and Sharla need you, and you need them. Please go back inside with them. It'll be easier on everybody if the three of you stick together."

"I can't go back in there!" Lionel screamed. "I can't do it! If I do, I'll, I'll …" That was the tipping point, and Carter couldn't miss the silent sob that shook Lionel's shoulders.

He didn't reach to touch the younger man, just stood there nearby. "It's okay to cry, son. When my dad died, I cried for days—I mean, *days*—and I didn't think I'd ever stop."

"Yeah, well, how old were you? Eight?"

"Nope. Thirty-two. I didn't have any brothers or sisters, so my dad and I were really close—my mom and I are too. I miss him every day."

"I never even knew my dad," the boy said, his head bowed.

"I know. But that's okay. You knew Tamara. You, Tamara, and Chelsea—you were sisters and brother. You've still got Chelsea, and she needs you, Lionel. Sharla does too. She's the closest thing to a mother you've got, and from what I can tell, a damn good one too."

"She is. She loves me and Tam. I knew that from the very start."

"Then go back in and cry *with* them. It'll be good for all of you to share that. Hell, sometimes I go to my mom's and we start talking about Dad and we *both* start crying. And it's okay. There's no shame in it, and there's no weakness there. Everybody has emotions, son. It's okay to let them out, especially with people who love you and feel the same way you do."

Lionel stood there for a full minute, not moving, and Carter wasn't sure if he'd gotten through to the kid or not. Finally, he turned, his face slick with tears. "Thank you, Sheriff Melton. Thanks for doing this for us."

"You're welcome, and call me Carter. That's my name, and I don't mind a bit. And if you need somebody to talk to, Lionel, a guy for, you know, guy stuff, my door is always open to you. Anytime. Not kidding. Always."

"Thanks." Lionel stood motionless for a few seconds before he said, "Guess I'd better get back in there." Carter held the door for him and waited until he entered, then followed him silently back to the door of the chapel.

There was still no one except Sharla and Chelsea inside when Lionel returned, and Carter realized they really *were* alone. They had no other family, just the three of them. When Lionel rejoined them, Sharla turned and motioned for Carter to come to her.

"You okay?" he asked as he neared her.

"Yeah. I thought maybe you'd want to come see her." Carter balked, but Sharla took his hand. "It's okay, Carter, really. I think she'd want you to be here just like we do." He still didn't want to step up to the casket, but he let Sharla lead him.

He'd seen her in the morgue, but there she'd just seemed like an object, something that someone was poking and prodding, something that was providing information for them. But there in the casket, dressed in a pale pink dress, hair and makeup done, she looked like a sleeping princess, her full lips blush pink and her hands resting lightly on her stomach. A pain shot through his chest as he took in her youth, cut short so unfairly, and he found his eyes starting to go blurry. "She looks beautiful, doesn't she?"

"She does. She really does." Carter stood there, overwhelmed with emotion, and finally stammered out, "Sharla, if there'd been any other way, if we'd had any other option, I promise you, we didn't want to—"

She pressed a slim finger to his lips to quiet him. "Shhhhh. We know that. You were doing what you had to do to survive. I don't know if she would've shot another one of you, but she'd already shot one, and you couldn't take that risk. Nobody blames you. Nobody. But I know you saw her out there in the weeds and stuff that night, in the dark, and in the morgue, and I wanted you to get a chance to see what a beautiful young woman she was."

"She really was," Carter said, still trying to rein in his feelings. God, what a shame! What a total and complete waste. *I'm gonna get the bastards who caused all this*, he promised himself in that moment. *They're gonna pay—I swear, they're gonna pay.* Hushed voices sounded from the back of the chapel and Carter turned to see Sam standing there with a woman who had to be Dahlia, his wife, and a tall, dark-haired man. "I need to go and speak with them. Will you be okay?"

"Sure. Go. Somebody you know?"

"Yeah. Reinforcements." He leaned in and whispered in her ear, "I'd love to kiss you and give you a big hug right now, and I can't, but I want you to know I would if I could."

"Same here," she whispered back. "And thanks again for being here and for talking to Lionel, because I know you did." A tiny smile turned the corners of her lips up, and he gave her a little fake salute before heading to the back.

"Hey, Carter, how's it going?" Sam said, grabbing his hand and shaking it.

"About as well as can be expected."

"Dahlia, this is the guy I was telling you about," Sam said with a grin.

"Good to meet you, Carter! Sam thinks a lot of you."

"That's good to know, I suppose! At least he's not calling me a son of a bitch behind my back!" Carter gave a little chuckle.

Sam turned to the other man. "Cruz, this is Carter Melton, sheriff of Trigg County. Carter, this is Cruz Livingston, FBI agent out of San Antonio, Texas."

"Great to meet you," Carter said, taking the man's hand.

Cruz's grip was strong and Carter noted his easy-going way of moving. "Great to meet you too. I hope this can be mutually beneficial."

"Let me take you up to meet the family. Come on." Carter headed up the aisle and straight to Sharla. "Ms. Barker, I'd like you to meet Detective Sam Curry of the Calloway County Sheriff's Department, and his wife, Dahlia."

Dahlia's voice was soft and soothing. "We're so sorry for your loss, Ms. Barker."

"Thank you. Were you there, Detective Curry?"

"I wasn't. But I know most of the men who were, and they're all grieving right along with your family, ma'am."

Sharla gave them what Carter thought of as a very brave smile, considering the circumstances. "Thank you."

"And this," Carter said, turning a bit toward Cruz, "is Agent Cruz Livingston of the FBI. Agent Livingston has come to give us some assistance in the case."

"Pleasure to meet you, ma'am, although I wish it were under different circumstances," Cruz said and took Sharla's hand.

"Thank you so much. But FBI?" Sharla gave them a quizzical look. "Is that really necessary?"

"It might be, ma'am, and I figured if I could assist, I would. But I'm very sorry for your loss, and I hope I can offer Sheriff Melton, Detective Curry, and the other fine members of the law enforcement community here with some assistance in figuring out what really happened that night." As he spoke, Carter listened. He liked this guy. Cruz was compassionate and genuine, and his demeanor would put anyone at ease. *We're going to work well together*, Carter thought. "I believe I'll just go out front for a little while before the service."

"I'll join you," Carter said, then gave Sharla a little nod before he followed Cruz down the aisle.

As soon as they cleared the front door, Cruz turned to Carter. "Something going on between the two of you?" Carter didn't know what to say. "Look, I can tell. I don't think anybody else can, but I can. I need everybody to be honest with me if this is going to work."

"Then yes. Something is going on between us. Something…"

"Romantic?" Carter nodded. "That's fine. She's a lovely woman and I can see how you'd be attracted to her. And I really don't think involvement with her is going to jeopardize this investigation, although if I were you, I'd keep it on the down low until this is over."

"That's exactly what we're doing," Carter assured him.

"Good. What's going on today?"

"Funeral. Burial. And I gave them a talking-to in the car, told them if they saw anything, anything at all, that gave them a feeling something was off, they should tell me. They understand."

"How much do they know?"

"They know there were drugs involved, but no particulars. They're the ones who told me about *La Tana del Lupo*, but they have no idea we know who or what that is. And the kids don't know about Sharla and me, but they will next week. We want to be honest with them, but careful at the same time."

"That's wise. Do you have more officers coming?"

"Yeah. This isn't my county, of course, but the sheriff here is a friend of mine and he's promised me some assistance in the way of eyes and boots on the ground."

Cruz nodded in understanding. "That's good. Very good. There's a real possibility that some over-zealous members of the public are going to show up. I'm probably going to be the only law enforcement in attendance who's not in identifying clothing of some kind, so I'm going to be available if needed. I'll just sit to the side in the rear and keep an eye out."

"That's what I was hoping you'd say. Listen, Cruz, thank you—thank you so much. You have no idea how much I appreciate this." Carter meant that. Just having Cruz there made him feel as if they had a chance at this thing, at bringing someone to justice over what happened with Tamara.

"I love a good mystery, and I've been wanting to see these guys taken down for a few years now. I've busted up drug-dealing motorcycle clubs and I don't mind going after these scumbags at all. Thanks for letting me come." The more Cruz talked, the more excited Carter got. They were really going to do this! Then Cruz asked the question Carter had been dreading: "Does the rest of law enforcement around here know that I'm involved? State police? State bureau of investigations?"

"No. Sam and I haven't told anybody. Can I be completely honest here?" Cruz nodded. "They treat us, sheriffs' departments and police departments, like red-headed stepchildren, like we're just bubbas who have no idea what we're doing, and we're all tired of it. I went to a meeting with all of them and I had more information to share than any of them did."

Cruz's brow furrowed. "Even though a trooper was killed?"

"Yeah. That's the shocking part. Anyway, I want these guys taken down. They've caused this family grief that was totally unnecessary and robbed the world of a special young person. Hell, maybe more than just her when we finally get down to it. I want them stopped cold."

"Then I'm gonna do whatever I can to help you," Cruz said and clapped Carter's shoulder with his big hand. "We'll get to the bottom of this. Meeting first thing in the morning?"

"You know it. I'll pick up coffee and donuts for everybody on the way, so you can pick out whatever you like best while we're there."

"Spoken like a true cop!" Cruz said, laughing, and Carter laughed too. It felt good to have something to laugh about, even if it was just for a minute.

Cars started to pull up, and Carter could only guess at their occupants. He and Cruz returned to the chapel, and he was pleased to see at least three deputies and two police officers from there in Hopkinsville. Good—they had backup if they needed it. As people came in, they signed the register and made their way up the aisle. They spoke to each other and the family in hushed tones, took Sharla and the kids' hands, patted their shoulders. Some he was sure were members of churches around there, most of them older people, and a few he was almost certain were faculty from the university. That made him smile. It was nice they cared enough to come.

One older man made his way over and when he reached Carter, he stopped and extended a hand. "Sheriff Melton?"

"Yes, sir. How may I help you?"

"My name is Professor Andrews. I was fortunate enough to have Miss Kent in my classes over the last three years. What an intelligent, promising young woman. Such a shame," the old gent said, hanging his head and shaking it.

"Yes, sir, it is. Very sad."

"I just spoke to Ms. Barker and she said to come to you. I think I may have some information you could use."

Carter perked up. A professor at the university? Yeah, he'd take any info the fellow might have. "Sir, thank you so much. I appreciate that. Could I give you a call and make a time to come and speak with you? I'll come to your home, or to the school, or wherever—"

"That would be fine. Perhaps we could meet halfway somewhere, if that would help."

"That would help greatly, sir. Thank you so much."

"Here." The man reached into a jacket pocket and handed Carter a business card. "Call anytime. If a woman answers, that's my wife. Tell her you're my bookie. She loves to get her hands on my cell phone, and I love to mess with her, if you know what I mean." Professor Andrews winked, and Carter liked the man immediately. Another piece of evidence! It was a terrible day, but good things were happening.

"I'll do that, sir! Thank you so much. I'll be in touch."

"Well, good day, young man. Pleasure meeting you." With that, the professor made his way to a pew and sat down beside a very attractive older lady. Carter glanced down at the business card: *Professor Aloysius T. Andrews, Ph.D.* Underneath that was *Chair, Biological Sciences Department.* Carter thought about college. God, he'd hated biology! He pocketed the card and looked around.

The chapel wasn't halfway full, but there was a good turnout for a Wednesday in the middle of the day. Movement caught his eye, and he watched one of the officers from the Hopkinsville Police Department take a woman by the arm and escort her out. It took him two seconds flat to get to the foyer, and the woman was arguing with the officer. "But I have a right to—"

"No, ma'am. This is a private service and you have

no right to be here. I'm going to have to ask you to leave."

Carter stopped short of them. "What's going on here?"

The woman wheeled on him and almost snarled. "I'm a reporter for the Christian County Gazette, and I wanted to interview the family but—"

"Absolutely *not*. I'm going to have to ask you to leave the premises," Carter announced.

She glared at his badge and then sneered. "And you have no jurisdiction here."

"I do, according to the sheriff of this county, who gave me jurisdiction this morning. You—leave. Now. Don't make me tell you a second time or I'll have you arrested for trespassing."

"This isn't a private gathering! It's open to the public!" the woman crowed.

A presence filled the little space around them and Carter was shocked when he heard that deep voice ask, "What's going on here?"

"I'm a member of the press and I—"

"Ma'am," Cruz said and pulled his credentials from his wallet, "I'm an agent with the FBI. There is an ongoing investigation into the circumstances surrounding the death of Miss Kent, and I'm going to have to ask you to leave or I'll be forced to arrest you for obstruction of justice."

"You wouldn't!" the young woman shouted.

"Please, ma'am, don't tell me what I will or won't do. The funeral will be over by the time your newspaper editor bails you out anyway. If I were you, I'd go right now before one of these fine officers loses his patience and puts you in cuffs."

"You can't do this!" she barked.

"Show a little decency, common courtesy, and respect, and get out of here," Carter snapped. It was about the most unprofessional thing he'd ever said and he didn't care one bit. All he really had on his mind at the moment was snapping the woman in half.

"I plan to report all of this!" she yelled as she slipped into her car.

"You go right ahead," Carter called back. He watched as she pulled out of the parking space, tires squealing, and that was when he heard it—a chuckle. He turned to find Cruz fighting laughter. "What? She's a bitch if there ever was one."

"You. Boy, you're like a rabid dog when it comes to protecting people! I like it, Carter, I really do. You and I are going to get along just fine," Cruz said, still grinning. "Come on. We need to get back inside."

"You couldn't really charge her with that, could you?" Carter asked with a smirk.

Cruz wore the best wise-ass face Carter had ever seen. "No, but she doesn't know that."

They all took their posts again and waited. The service was very nice. One of the members of the faculty at the university conveyed the condolences of the entire campus. Lionel read a poem he and Tamara had written together when they were just children. A local minister stood and talked about forgiveness, about how it benefitted the person giving it as much as the person receiving it. As they spoke, one of the funeral home employees came by and whispered to Carter that the other law enforcement officers there were going to run traffic interference for the funeral procession, and that the family had requested he drive them to the cemetery. That suited him just fine, and he gave the man the keys to his cruiser so it could be moved up into the funeral procession.

He met them at the back door and helped all three of them into the car, then followed the hearse to the cemetery, taking that time to remind them once again to report anything they saw that caught their eye as being off in any way. Once there, he and Sam escorted the family to the chairs under the tent, then took up spots around the perimeter, along with the other officers who'd been at the funeral home. He was glad to see Cruz wander up and take up a position opposite his own.

The minister began to speak and Carter was lost in the droning of his voice, deep in thought about Tamara, his dad, and his grandparents, when he detected movement and turned. It was Chelsea. As soon as she caught his eye, she mouthed something. Carter couldn't make it out, but he didn't want to show any outward signs, so he just raised one eyebrow slightly. Chelsea caught his expression and repeated it as Carter stared at her lips. *Free? Breeze?* Still not understanding, he watched again, and that time he got it: *Trees.* As he gave her a slight nod, she tipped her head back in the opposite direction. Not wanting to draw attention, Carter turned his back to the area she'd indicated and sent a quick text to Cruz: *The daughter says there's someone in the tree line to your right.* When he turned back, he saw Cruz give him a glance that told him the message was received. The agent moved slowly but steadily, weaving his way through the crowd and heading to the left, then stealthily moving around to circle to the back of the tent where no one was standing. Carter knew he'd hug close to the tent and try to get a look at whatever Chelsea was seeing.

He'd never seen anybody sprint like that from a dead run, but Cruz's long legs covered the distance between the tent and the tree line at a remarkable speed, and in seconds Carter and Sam both were on the move too, running as fast as they could toward the brush. It was all in vain. From a distance, Carter could hear the sound of a car door slamming and tires slinging gravel. They weren't fast enough. When he reached the clearing on the other side, Cruz and Sam stood there, hands on their thighs, sucking in air. "Did you see the car?" Carter asked, breathless.

Cruz shook his head. "No. He was gone by the time we got here."

"Damn it! So close …" Carter closed his eyes. No, no, no. They needed whoever it was.

"It's okay. He knows somebody was on to him, and he'll go back and tell whoever he's working for or with. And that's okay. We want them to know we're looking. They'll trip up and it'll be easier to catch them. Good work, guys," Cruz said and slapped Carter and Sam on the back.

They made their way to the tree line and stood there just at its edge, hesitant to disrupt the service any more than they already had. Sharla, Chelsea, and Lionel stood and dropped long-stemmed roses into the grave, and with the final prayer, the service was over. Attendees were shaking hands with the family and encouraging them, but Carter was concerned. Sharla's drawn, ashen face looked totally and completely worn out. All he wanted was to get them back to the funeral home to pick up the food and then home to eat so they could rest. After telling Sam where the extra key was so he could drop Cruz off at the house, he gathered up Sharla, Chelsea, and Lionel and led them to the car.

He waited until he pulled out on the highway before he asked the question. "Chelsea, who did you see?"

"That was the guy who was doing the rally! I recognized him!"

"The one speaking and talking about arming yourselves?"

"No. This one was off to the side, but he was acting like he was running the show. I saw him telling the other guys what to do. And he was handing those bandages to kids to take around and pass out to people with the tattoos. There were copies of the tattoo, and he was giving them to people to pass out. It was like he was the boss or something."

"Do you think you could describe him to a police sketch artist?"

She stared up at the car's headliner for a few seconds before she answered. "Yeah. Maybe. I don't know how that works, but I'd be willing to try it."

"Okay. We don't have one, but I know a few places that do. If I have to, I'll take you to Nashville to get somebody down there to do it. We'll find *somebody*, but anything you can give us will help."

"Sheriff Melton? Who was that—"

"Carter. Call me Carter."

The girl nodded. "Okay. Carter, who was that guy? The tall one? Dark hair? Very good looking?"

He hadn't intended to tell the two college students, but he wasn't going to let their question go unanswered. "That's Cruz Livingston. He's an FBI agent from Texas."

Lionel sat straight up in the back seat. "FBI? Really? All the way from Texas?" Carter nodded. "Wow. This must really be serious."

"It is. Two people died. That's pretty damn serious. The blond man talking to me this afternoon? That's Detective Curry from the Calloway County Sheriff's Department. His wife used to be FBI, and she worked with Agent Livingston. She called him and told him about the case, and he wanted to help."

"That's pretty amazing, really, if you think about it," Chelsea said, musing aloud. "To be so far away and be interested in coming here to help us."

"Actually, he thinks this might relate to a case they've worked on," Carter said as off-handedly as possible. No way did he want to answer questions about that.

"Oh. I see. Well, anyway, he's here, and that's great. And Mom, hey, he's hot! You should get to know him!"

Carter glanced over at Sharla and saw her smile. "Nah. I'm already spoken for."

Lionel spoke up. "What are you talking about? You haven't seen anybody in years! That last guy, what was his name? Prick?" Chelsea started to laugh, and Carter couldn't help but join in.

Sharla cried out, "No! His name was Pratt."

"Well, he was a prick," Lionel insisted.

"I'd call him more of a jerk," Chelsea said. "Or a dick."

"What are you laughing about?" Sharla almost yelled at Carter.

"Nothing. I'm not laughing," Carter said, then busted out in guffaws again.

"It's not funny! But he was kinda a dick," Sharla grumbled.

Chelsea just wouldn't let it go. "So go after Agent Livingston! What have you got to lose?"

Carter couldn't help himself. "Me."

Chelsea and Lionel both gave him the side-eye, and Chelsea squeaked out, "What?"

"Me. She'd lose me."

The girl screwed up her face. "What are you talking about?"

"You want to tell them or shall I?" Carter asked,

turning to look at Sharla there, her face red from stifling laughter.

"Oh, what the hell. Carter and I have been seeing each other."

There was silence in the car. Finally, just as Carter was thinking he'd have to say *something*, Lionel said, "I guess you could do a lot worse."

Two seconds later, they were all laughing so hard that Carter had to pull off the street and into a parking lot. "Wow, glowing endorsement you got there from Li," Chelsea said through her laughter.

"Yeah. Don't be too enthusiastic, Lionel, okay? You might hurt yourself," Carter told him, still laughing.

"Oh, I'm just messing with you. You're a pretty good guy, for a cop," Lionel added, and the laughter started all over again.

"This was *not* how I'd planned to do this," Sharla said as they all quieted down.

"Yeah, but it's how it happened, so that's just how it is. And I want you two to know," he said, catching Chelsea and Lionel's gazes in the rear view mirror, "that I love and respect Sharla, and I want to get to know both of you and have a good relationship with you because you're important to her *and* you're good people."

Chelsea was the first to speak. "Mom, if you're going to see somebody, I'm glad it's Sher … Carter."

"Yeah. I feel the same way," Lionel threw in.

"Thanks. That means a lot to me," Carter told them. "Now let's get this food home and get you all settled for the evening. You need to get some rest. We'll talk about the guy in the woods tomorrow."

Twenty minutes later, everyone was safe and sound, the food was eaten and put away, and goodbyes were said. Sharla walked Carter to the car and when they reached it, she grabbed both sides of his belt and pulled him toward her. "Kiss me goodnight?"

"You bet." His arms encircled her and he drew her in snug against him as he kissed her gently. "I love you, Sharla. I hope I helped a little bit today," he whispered against her cheek.

"It helped enormously. You can't know how much. I love you, Carter. Thanks for everything. Talk to you tomorrow?"

"You bet. Get some sleep. Night." As he pulled away, he looked back and could see Chelsea and Lionel watching out the window. They'd seen him kiss her.

And that was perfectly okay with him.

CHAPTER 7

His alarm went off like always, and Carter sat up. When he'd come in the night before, there'd been a note on the table: *Gone on to bed. I hate flying. Talk to you in the morning.* He'd stopped at the guest room's door and he could hear Cruz sawing logs. Good thing the house was old and had thick walls.

He started a pot of coffee and made his way to the sofa. With the sound turned way down on the TV, he watched morning headlines on a news show on his streaming service, then checked his mail from the day before. Bill. Bill. Advertisement. AARP. They'd been pursuing him since he was twenty, and he wasn't sure why. He was a long way from their membership requirements. Well, not a *long* way, but long enough.

"Mornin'," a voice said in a Texas drawl and Carter looked up to see Cruz shuffle out of the bedroom.

"Hot coffee and donuts, as promised," Carter said, pointing over his shoulder toward the kitchen.

"Thanks, man. Anything going on in the big wide world?"

"Nah. Auto workers' strike. Middle Eastern country dropping bombs in another Middle Eastern country, and us planning to get right in the middle of it. So much for minding our own business. Oh, and somebody sent some white powder to the White House again."

"Fucking assholes. They get everybody in an uproar and it turns out to be a hoax. Do they have any idea how much of the taxpayers' money they waste with that stupid shit?" Cruz asked, and Carter chuckled.

"If they know, they don't care."

"Yeah. It's all about them." He heard Cruz take a slurp of coffee and since he didn't spit it across the room, it must've been to his liking.

"Oh, by the way, I asked Chelsea if she thought she could work with a police sketch artist to get us a drawing of the person she saw yesterday. She said he was at the rally, and he seemed—"

"Stop right there. Didn't want to say anything in front of everybody else, but I saw him and I know who he is," Cruz said, plopping down on the sofa after setting his cup on the coffee table.

"You do?"

"Yup." He took another slurping sip and set the cup down again. "Name's Paul Angelico. Actually, Paolo. Funny name for Satan incarnate, Angelico. They call him *Capo Paolo*. Means Boss Paul in Italian."

"I take it he's the head of this *La Tana del Lupo*?"

"Yes. And if he's here, there's got to be a really good reason."

"The rally?"

"No. More than that. It's got to be big. Something very important." Both men sat there, staring into their coffee cups. "I mean, I have no idea what, but he didn't just happen to hold a rally here. Do you know if there have been any anywhere else?"

"We've had zero luck finding out anything about the campus group." Carter took another sip of coffee and balanced the cup on his thigh. "What are you thinking?"

"I don't know yet, but something's bothering me. Let's get to the office and let me dig into what you've got."

They stepped into the office in less than forty-five minutes, ready for the day. Edwards and Durst were getting ready to head out, and Lewis and Watson were scheduled to come in at three. After introductions, the two deputies left and Carter and Cruz were alone to work.

The small storage area turned conference room was all Carter had, so they spread everything out on the table and started going through it piece by piece. When he got to the robbery, Cruz stopped him. "So do you know where these guys are?"

"Yeah. High sec, fed lodging, Pennington Gap, Virginia."

"Life?"

"Yeah."

"Have you requested their records?"

That hadn't even occurred to Carter. "No, but I will."

"Don't. We'll go there. O'Fallon, Missouri?" Carter nodded. "We can drive there, right?"

"Yeah. About three and a half hours."

"Good. We need to do that. Call them and let them know we're coming and what we'll need."

"Will do."

"Okay. Keep going."

It took another hour, but Carter got through everything they had. "Oh, and I got this last night." He pulled out the business card and held it up. "Professor at the university. He said he might have some information on the group."

"That's good, seeing as how we have nothing up to now. I've been thinking about it, Carter." Cruz stared him in the eyes, and Carter was pretty sure he wasn't going to like what the agent had to say. "We need to let everybody know I'm here. We won't get anywhere if I ruffle feathers."

"I was afraid you were going to say that. I'm also afraid you're right."

"I'll let you handle that. We can have a get-together and you can introduce me, or you can just let them run into me as we go, but they need to at least know I'm here."

"I'll handle it. I don't want to put you in a difficult position."

Cruz smiled. "They won't like me being here, but

they'll have to live with it. As long as we figure this out, I don't care if they like me and want me here or not. Doesn't matter. I'm here to do a job. But there's no quicker way to make an enemy than to blindside somebody."

Carter nodded. He'd hoped to keep Cruz as his ace in the hole, but the agent was right and Carter was just being juvenile about it. Yeah, they were looked down upon by the "big boys," but he was confident in his ability to do his job and do it well. Why should he care what they thought? "I'll shoot out an email, let everybody know you're here and what your role will be. I'll also call the police department in O'Fallon and let them know we're going to be coming to go through the records." As he spoke, he wondered how he was going to do everything he needed to do as sheriff and still work on the case.

He hadn't realized he was sitting still and silent when Cruz's voice broke into his thoughts. "Carter?" Lifting his head, he let Cruz catch his gaze and hold it. "Listen to me. I'm here to *help*. While you're working on this, you're also the sheriff of this county. You've got deputies depending on you, and you've got the residents of a county who expect you to be on your toes. I'm not going to lock you out of anything or keep anything from you. Anything I learn, you'll know about. Can you do that?"

"Yes. Thank you." Carter felt like his head was going to explode. So much to do, so little time, and he felt so pressured.

"Good. I'll go to the university and talk to the professor. Call him and tell him you're sending me, and I'm sure he'll be fine with it. While I'm gone, call O'Fallon. Also, check to see if the prison where those guys are will let us visit because after we read their records, we may want to go there."

"True. I'll call them."

"Now, do me a favor. Call Sharla and take her to dinner. Try to relax a little. Have a couple of drinks, dance, and have a pleasant evening. I'll call you when I finish with the professor, and then I'll make dinner plans with Sam and Dahlia before I come back. I'll be back long before you are and, trust me, I can entertain myself. Do it, Carter. Take a deep breath. We've got this, bud."

The kindness in Cruz's eyes was a salve to Carter's battered soul. It was okay. Things were going to be fine. Someone besides him and Sam was taking up the torch, and it would all be okay.

An hour later, he'd been told by the prison that they could announce their intention to visit as late as six hours beforehand, and the O'Fallon Police Department said they'd welcome the two law enforcement officers anytime. Maybe they'd get some answers soon. He remembered Sharla's face from the day before, tired and puffy. That was how his brain felt.

But he was pretty sure everything would be fine in her arms.

* * *

"I'M SO TIRED. CAN WE JUST STAY IN?" SHARLA WHINED into the phone.

That made Carter sigh. So much for having a fun, relaxing evening. Then he realized if they did that, they could sit around in pajamas. That would be *very* relaxing. "Okay. Want me to come there, or do you want to come here?"

"Can I come there? I won't feel so pressured to run the washing machine or empty the dishwasher."

"Sure. Bring clothes so you can go straight to work. That'll save you time, babe."

"I will. I'll be there in a bit. Love you, Carter."

"Love you too, baby. Be careful."

Carter thought about it. Would it bother Cruz for Sharla to be there? Probably not. They were all adults. What did he need to do before she got there? Nothing. There were coffee cups in the sink and his sheets needed to be changed, but other than that, the house was in good shape. He paid Angie Proctor to clean once a week, and she'd always done a good job. It was almost time to go home, and he wrote up notes for the guys leaving and those coming in. Everything was almost done when the door opened and he looked up.

Penny Tadlock. *Well, fuck me*, Carter thought. "There you are, Sheriff Melton! I haven't seen you in forever!" she cooed as she waved to him.

Carter got up from the big common desk and went to the counter. "How are you, Penny?"

"I'm fine! Thank you for asking! And how are you?"

"Quite well, thanks. What can I help you with?"

"I was wondering what you were doing next Tuesday. I'm having a little get-together at my house, and thought you might want to come."

"I doubt I'd be able to, but thanks for inviting me."

"Oh, but I'd love for you to be there! Could you please think about it?"

Hit it, Carter thought. "Well, I'd have to talk to my girlfriend and see what she's got planned."

Penny's face paled and her jaw dropped before she finally sputtered, "Your, your, your *girlfriend*?"

"Yep. I mean, I can't go to a party unaccompanied and leave her behind."

"Well, uh, I only have spots for, um, for so many people, and I, um, hadn't planned—"

"Oh, that's all right. Thanks for inviting me though. Maybe next time you can plan it so I can bring her." It was all Carter could do to keep a straight face. He was dying from laughter on the inside, and he hoped she couldn't see it in his eyes.

"Uh, yeah, okay. That's, um, I can do that. So, uh, have a good evening and I'll be seeing you, Sheriff Melton. You take care now." He didn't get a chance to say another word before she hustled herself out the front door and down the block.

"Well, fiddle-dee-dee. Invited and uninvited in under five minutes. Good work, Melton," he told himself with glee. Now maybe that trouble on feet would stay away from him!

He hadn't been home ten minutes when he heard a car in the drive. When he snapped the door open,

Sharla stood there, her fist raised to rap on the door. Carter let out a laugh. "Gonna punch me in the nose?"

"No, silly." She stepped inside and closed the door behind her. "If I were going to do that, you wouldn't still be upright." Then she gave him a quick peck on the lips.

"Oh, is that right?" Before she could answer, Carter grabbed her and locked his lips to hers. Their tongues had been thrashing around for a full minute when he pulled back. "As you can see, I'm terrified of you."

"Absolutely terrified, and you should be. So how was your day?"

"Got a lecture from Cruz on playing well with others," Carter said and pulled a beer out of the refrigerator. "Want one?"

"Please." He popped the top on the one he was holding, handed it to her, and retrieved another for himself. Following her back into the living room, he waited until she'd dropped onto the sofa, and he followed her lead and plopped down beside her. "What was this lecture about?"

"Telling the other agencies that he's here and working with us. I didn't want to, but I will."

She gave him a stern glare from under her brows. "You know that's the right thing to do."

"Yeah, but I didn't want to. Guess that's kinda childish, huh?"

"A little bit."

"But he's in Murray talking to the professor. I about halfway expect him to call at any minute. We're also

161

going to O'Fallon to look at the records of the two guys who were involved in the robbery with Taliq."

"That's a good idea."

"And I called the prison to make sure we could visit if we think we need to."

"Also a good idea."

"And your day?"

"Dealing with a little lady who has pneumonia. Poor little thing. She's like eighty-three and very weak. I helped her with some breathing treatments, but I'm afraid the evening shift won't keep up with them and she won't be any better in the morning."

"That's awful."

Sharla nodded. "Yeah. She's so sweet."

"Get the kids back to school?"

"Yeah. They didn't want to go, but I told them it was best to stay busy."

"Yep. Probably." His phone rang and he looked at the screen. "Cruz. Gotta take it. Hey, bud, any luck?"

"A little. Before you grill me, I recorded the whole conversation on my phone so you can listen to it. That way you might pick up on something I missed and vice versa. O'Fallon? Prison?"

"Yes and yes. Anytime we want."

"Good and good. I'm on my way to Sam and Dahlia's right now and we're going to some buffet here that they like. Don't know how late I'll be."

"That's okay. Sharla's here with me and she's staying the night. Hope that doesn't bother you."

A snicker rolled out of the phone. "Bother me? The

way I snore, I doubt I'd hear anything if you were tearing the house down!"

"I take it that's a no!" Carter said, laughing.

"Your house, your girlfriend. You staying in?"

"Yeah, she's begging to. We're both exhausted."

"I know. I could see that in your face. I'd hoped you'd have some fun, but you need the rest. Hang in there. It's going to get better. Just wait until tomorrow. Today I went over your stuff. Tomorrow you go through mine."

"Good!"

"Yeah. I've got some stuff that you haven't ..." Carter was trying to listen, but the sound of keys in the lock startled him and he sat straight up. The door cracked open just a little and he heard something he never dreamed he'd hear.

"Hello? Carter? Son? It's Mom. Are you here, honey?"

"Jesus, Cruz, sorry to interrupt, but I'll have to talk to you later. Small emergency. Bye." *Shit! What is she doing here?* Carter wanted to scream. "Mom?"

"Hi, honey! I cooked a bunch of chicken and mashed potatoes and gravy and ... Well, hello! Who do we have here?" Wilda Fern asked, eyes wide and a huge casserole dish in her hands.

"Um, Mom, this is my friend, Sharla Barker. Sharla, this is my mother, Wilda Fern Melton."

"Here, let me take that for you," Sharla said and reached for the dish. Wilda Fern handed it off, that dumbfounded look still on her face, and watched silently as Sharla disappeared into the kitchen.

"Carter?"

"Mom, I didn't want you to find out this way, but Sharla and I have been seeing each other for a little while now."

"Oh. Well, you know how it is. The mom's always the last to know," Wilda Fern huffed.

"Don't be like that. I just hadn't had a chance to talk to you."

"Did I miss anything?" Sharla asked as she rejoined them, a huge smile on her face.

"No, babe. I was just telling Mom that we've been seeing each other for a little while and I hadn't had a chance to tell her yet."

"Oh, yes, Mrs. Melton. Carter was just saying to me that he needed to introduce us." Sharla held out a hand, which Wilda Fern took hesitantly. "It's so good to meet you."

Dear god, woman, if I loved you before, I love you ten times more now, Carter wanted to sing. She'd just saved his ass and said the absolute best thing she could've said. "That's right, Mom. We decided we wanted to have some quiet, alone time tonight. Sharla lost a family member and she's had a rough week."

Wilda Fern tipped her head and frowned. "Oh, sweetie, I'm so sorry! I hope you're doing okay."

"Yes, ma'am, thank you. I am, thanks to this wonderful son of yours. You sure did a good job raising him."

Oh my god, she's going to send me to a commune and

keep you! Carter was trying not to laugh. Boy, Sharla was pouring it on thick and his mother was lapping it up! He almost laughed out loud when Wilda Fern said, "Well, I did my best."

The smile Sharla gave his mother was a mile wide. "You did good. Would you care for something to drink?"

"Um, no thanks. It never occurred to me that you might ... What I meant was ... If I'd known ..." Wilda Fern fumbled for words, which made it even harder for Carter to keep a straight face.

He couldn't help it—he had to poke the bear. "So is there enough for two, Mom? Because if not, I'm going to have to find something else for us to eat."

"Oh, yes. I brought enough for you to eat for a couple of days, so there should be plenty. I'm sure glad I did this. You'll enjoy it." She stood there for a few seconds as though she didn't know what to do before she said, "Well, okay, I'll be going now. Y'all have a pleasant evening."

"It was nice to meet you, Mrs. Melton."

"Nice to meet you too, dear. Carter, honey, will you walk me out?"

"Sure, Mom." *Oh, hell. Here we go with the third degree,* Carter's inner child groused.

They'd no more than made it out the door before the questions started. "So, how did you two meet?"

"Through work." That was a good-enough answer.

"And what does she do for a living?"

"She's a respiratory therapist in Hopkinsville."

"Oh!" She seemed genuinely surprised he hadn't said she was an exotic dancer or prostitute or something, or at least that's what Carter imagined. "So, is she divorced or widowed?"

"Divorced. For a long, long time."

"Oh."

It would be nice if she'd just stop there, but there's no way she's going to do that, Carter told himself, and he was right.

"Son, do you have protection?"

It took everything Carter had not to roll his eyes. "Mom, I'm forty-two years old. If I don't know how to take care of myself by now, I never will."

"Well, you can't be too safe, you know."

"Yes. I'm aware. But I need to get in here and eat before it gets cold, right? That's what you always say, isn't it?"

"Well, um, yes, it is. Okay. So I'll be going now. But I'll call you, okay?"

"Okay, Mom. Thanks so much for the food. I know we'll enjoy it. Bye." He backed away, waving, and hoped she'd take the hint. Sure enough, she climbed into her car, waved, and drove away. Carter practically ran to the house and slammed the door closed behind himself. "Oh my god."

Sharla stood in the kitchen doorway, laughing hysterically. "Okay, that was the most entertaining thing I've seen in a long, long time! She's a hoot!"

"When we got outside, she asked me if I had protection."

Sharla doubled over. "She did not! Oh my god, I can't breathe!"

"I know, right?"

"What did you tell her?"

"I told her I'm forty-two years old and if I can't take care of myself by now, there's no hope."

"Yeah, no shit. I hope you don't mind, but I got out plates and filled them. The food's ready to eat, and I have to say, it smells delicious."

"My mom's a lot of things, but one of the best ones is that she's a great cook."

They sat in the little kitchen and enjoyed the food. Wilda Fern had always been a spectacular cook. No, there were no exotic Indian or French dishes, and she'd never made a soufflé in her life, but she was the queen of good home cookin', and Carter loved everything that came from her kitchen.

As they ate, he wanted desperately to ask Sharla about Imogen and Taliq, but he wasn't sure how to go about it. They were, after all, supposed to be having a quiet evening. Then, out of the blue, she started the conversation, and Carter couldn't believe how lucky he'd gotten with that.

"So you have no siblings?"

Carter shook his head. "No. Only child."

"And your dad passed?"

"Yeah. About fifteen years ago. Cancer."

"Oh, that's rough, and I should know. Lost both of my parents to it."

"That *is* rough," Carter murmured.

"And my sister."

"Even rougher."

"Yeah. She was thirty-three. Two years older than me. Tamara was thirteen and Lionel was eleven. It was hard, taking two almost-grown kids and trying to be their mother, not to mention having one of my own who was nine."

"I admire you greatly for that."

"Don't. I did what anybody else would've done."

"Maybe not. That was hard. Taliq was killed when Tamara was three and Lionel wasn't even one. Imogen was the problem child, always pushing the limits, always giving my parents fits. She told me once that the only reason she'd gotten involved with Taliq was because she knew our parents would be pissed when they found out she was seeing a person of another race. He came from a very nice family, and she said his parents had been kind to her and seemed to like her, but she had no idea why he turned out to be a no-good piece of shit from the get-go. Had nothing to do with his color and everything to do with his nasty personality. He beat on her, pushed her around, and she let him. We were lucky Tamara barely remembered him, and Lionel never knew him. But other than that, Imogen was a good mother. She loved those kids. All she worried about the whole time she was sick was what would happen to them, even though I assured her I'd take care of them, seeing as how our parents and Taliq's were gone."

"And that hasn't been easy," Carter said, smoothing

her hair with a gentle hand, then cupping her jaw. "You're an amazing woman."

"Not really. I just worked. I got up every day and put one foot in front of the other. When the cancer became too advanced, she came to live with me because she couldn't take care of herself or hold a job. That was *really* hard."

"I guess Taliq left her with nothing, right?"

"You know, it's funny you'd say that. He told her over and over that he had an insurance policy, but she never found anything. Nothing. So I have no idea what he was talking about. After she died, I went through all her personal stuff, thinking maybe I'd find something, but I never did."

"Nothing?"

"Nope. But she kept journals, and it was nice to read some of the things she'd written. Some of it was hard, though, when she wrote about the things Taliq did to her, the beatings and how she felt so alone and helpless. Of course, she could've come to me or, until they died, our parents, but she wouldn't."

"That's a shame."

"Yes. It was. I loved my sister, but she was stubborn and hard-headed. God, she was so beautiful, but she was so conceited! I mean, I guess I'm okay looking, but Imogen was a knock-out."

"Okay? Babe, you're beautiful. The first time I saw you I thought, wow, if I could just get to know that woman. I never dreamed you'd give me a second glance."

"Give you a second glance? Carter, panties burst into flames when you walk past a lingerie department! Don't you notice how women look at you?"

Carter was confused. "Women look at me?"

"Look at you? They leave a trail of drool behind them."

He laughed aloud. "They do not!"

"Oh, yes, they do."

Without even thinking, he whispered, "Penny Tadlock."

"Who?"

"Oh, nobody. Just … nobody, really. But seriously, women don't look at me that way."

"Yes, Carter, they do. All the time."

"Well, it won't do them any good because I'm taken." He grinned at her. "They can't have me. I'm all yours."

"If you're all mine, then let's get this kitchen cleaned up so I can enjoy what's all mine, how's about it, stud?" She wiggled her eyebrows and Carter laughed at her.

"Stud, huh? I'll show you stud! We can clean up the kitchen in the morning! Get in that bedroom, woman!"

"No. We've got to clean up our mess and then we can make one in your bed. Come on. Help me out here," she said, rising and taking dishes to the sink.

An hour later, as he stroked into her, Carter looked down into those big, luminous, blue eyes and smiled. "I love you, beautiful girl," he whispered and leaned down to nip her lips before he dropped a kiss onto them.

"And I love you too, my hero."

My hero. He wanted to be her hero, and he had a lot

of work to do to get there. But he made himself a silent promise right that minute. She'd be safe, she and those two kids, sheltered from the pain of neglect and poverty. They'd never be hurt or abandoned again. They'd never be alone. He'd see to it.

Still, he'd never say that out loud to her. It was better not to make a promise if you weren't sure you could keep it. At that point, everything was up for grabs. They had to get some kind of fruitful lead soon. He hoped lives didn't depend on it.

* * *

"You didn't tell me Cruz was staying here!" Sharla whispered as she slipped back into bed beside him.

Carter rolled toward her in the early-morning darkness. "I thought I did."

"No. You didn't. I went in the kitchen to get a bottle of water and ran right into him as he came out of the bathroom."

That made him sit straight up in bed. "Oh, shit! You weren't ..." He threw the covers back—tee shirt. "Thank god you weren't naked."

"Yeah, no shit. That would've been awkward, to say the least." She reached for him as he fell back into the pillows and he rolled to face her. Her fingers combed through his hair and she smiled. "I like this." Snuggling down beside him, she threw an arm over him and he kissed the top of her head.

"I like it too. We've got tonight and then the kids

will be home for the weekend, so we'll have to … Wait. They know." Carter grinned. "We don't have to sneak around."

"Yeah, but we can't be having wild monkey sex with them in the house."

"True."

"So what's on your agenda for today?"

"I don't know, but I have this feeling Cruz is going to want to go to O'Fallon, which is fine with me."

Sharla nodded against the pillow. "Okay. So don't hold dinner. Is that the message there?"

"Probably." He rested his cheek against the crown of her head and sighed. *Here we go*, he thought grimly. *Pretty soon it's going to be fussing about why I'm not home for dinner, why I have to work on Sunday, why we can't have a holiday together. And then it'll be over.* He knew that. It was a surety. And yet there he was, trying to forge a relationship and believe Sharla would be different. It wasn't about her being a woman. It was about her being a partner in a relationship where it seemed she was the only one giving anything, and that was exactly how she'd start to see it. It was simply a matter of time.

Just as he started to say something along those lines, the alarm clock went off. *Saved by the bell*, he told himself as he slapped the top of the damn thing. "Time to make the coffee. I sure hope you brought something to wear as bottoms."

"Yoga pants."

"Good. At least you can get around in the house

without having to be fully dressed." The coffee pot was calling him, and he left Sharla sitting in the bed, rubbing her eyes.

By the time the coffee was done, Cruz was standing in the kitchen, mug in hand. "You up for O'Fallon today?" he asked as Carter reached up into the cabinet to retrieve mugs for himself and Sharla.

"I told her that's probably what you were going to ask about, and yeah, I'm up for it."

"Good. Let's go that way. I can fill you in on the professor's info in the car on the way. And pack a bag. If this takes longer than we think, we can get a room and start again tomorrow."

As soon as Sharla left for work, Carter packed his little duffel and dropped it by the front door. In fifteen minutes, they were on the road, and in thirty-five, they were crossing the state line in Wickliffe, Kentucky, into Cairo, Illinois, to catch I-57 and connect to I-55, their direct route into St. Louis. It was mostly farming country, not a lot to see, and they chatted as Carter drove. Once they were finally settled on I-55, Cruz pulled out his phone. "Let's listen to the recording and see if you catch anything I didn't." Linking his phone with Carter's Bluetooth device in the car, Cruz hit PLAY and the space was filled with the professor's voice.

As soon as it finished, Carter snorted. "Well, there *are* people on campus who know about that group."

"Yeah, and the school's been accepting donations in order to let it meet on campus without appropriate sponsorship or paperwork. Wonder if they're taking personal kickbacks?"

"Our department doesn't have the ability to look into financial records, but—"

"On it." Cruz spent the next five minutes talking to someone on his phone. Carter wasn't sure who it was, and he didn't really feel the need to ask. The job was getting done, and that was all he cared about. When Cruz hung up, he stared at Carter. "Do you think there's anybody in the sheriff's office or city police department in Murray who knows about this?"

"I doubt it. If there were, Sam would have some inkling of it, and he's said nothing. I really believe in an officer's intuition, and I think he would've picked up on it if that were the case."

"Yeah, probably. So I've got one of the analysts in my office working on getting into the financials of the university. It's a public institution, so that makes it easier, and with the name of the school's contact, James Goodall, we've got somewhere to look for personal gain too. By the way," Cruz asked, "did you send out that email?"

Carter pointed to his phone. "Sure did. Wanted to copy you but I didn't have your email addy. Grab my phone, open my email, and look in my sent file." He'd worked on the email for a few minutes before sending it because he wanted it just right, and he was pretty sure he'd nailed it.

TO: All involved investigative entities, Palmer slaying
FROM: Carter Melton, Sheriff, Trigg County, KY

RE: Welcome to Cruz Livingston

As of today's date, we have assistance from Agent Cruz Livingston, FBI out of Texas. Agent Livingston is a personal friend of Detective Sam Curry, Calloway County SD, and in conversation was alerted to the possibility that the FBI has detected a connection between the Palmer shooting and organized gang activity in their district. As a professional courtesy, Agent Livingston has been allowed to assist us in our investigation. I know you all will welcome him, as we can always use additional assistance, especially when it comes at no cost to our already-burdened department budgets. Agent Livingston is staying at my house as a courtesy to his department. Please feel free to contact him if you would like to speak to him about his knowledge of the case. Thank you.

"Perfect. Just what they need to know and nothing more. I like it. And you included my number at the bottom, which I'm glad you did. If they want to know something, they can contact me directly and won't have to bother you."

"Transparency. That's what I was aiming for, transparency on a need-to-know basis."

"Yep. Exactly." Cruz settled back into the passenger seat again and they rode along, occasionally commenting on something on the side of the road.

They hit Cape Girardeau, Missouri, at lunchtime, so they stopped and ate, then got back on the road. From there, it wasn't long before they were greeted with a sign that read, *O'Fallon City Limits*, and a population estimate. Not a big place, but it was a bedroom community of St. Louis, so that estimation didn't mean much. It wasn't hard to find their municipal building and in minutes, Carter and Cruz were checking in at the front desk and being led to the court clerk's office.

"Looks like you'd better be glad I told you to pack a bag," Cruz whispered as they carried the boxes of files down the hallway. "These two guys were obviously very note-worthy."

"Yeah, looks that way. This is going to take forever."

"You'd better tell your girlfriend you're going to be tied up for a while," Cruz said with a wink.

"I thought I told her you were going to be there last night, but she said I didn't. She was really embarrassed about running into you in the hallway."

Cruz laughed aloud. "No biggie! She had on a tee and panties, and I was wearing my boxer briefs. It's not like we were naked!"

"That's exactly what I told her!" Carter said, laughing, as Cruz backed the conference room door open and they plopped the boxes down on the desk.

And so they started. It was ridiculous. There was motion after motion trying to get the discovery thrown out, trying to get evidence thrown out, trying to get the court dates changed here and there, and worse yet, several motions to dismiss. All were denied, obviously. They'd been at it for about ten minutes when Carter choked out, "Wait! What the hell? This is dated six months prior to the robbery."

Cruz looked over what was in his hand. "Yeah. This is dated four months prior. Holy shit. We're in the wrong place. We should be at the police station."

"Sure looks that way. What should we do with this stuff?"

"Leave it. Tell them we'll be back. If we don't need it, we'll come back and tell them. But we need to see what the department has on these guys." Cruz stood and headed out the conference room door, Carter right on his heels.

The police station was down the block. They'd asked the court clerk's office to call ahead, and there was a sergeant waiting for them when they arrived. When they told him what they wanted, he shook his head. "Bad news. I was here the first time they were arrested."

"First time, huh?" Carter stared at him. "What are we talking about here?"

"Oh, just wait," the sergeant, whose name they'd learned was Langstaff, said with a smirk. "You're in for a *real* treat. Hope you've got some time on your hands." Carter didn't see that as a good sign.

And he was right in his guess. There were two big boxes of files, not to mention a list of evidence a mile long. He wasn't feeling too much trepidation about it until Langstaff toted in another box, and then another. "What are these?"

"All of the robberies."

"Wait." Cruz wheeled and stared at the sergeant. "There was more than one?"

"Four. Four armed robberies. Same three guys. I told you it would be a real treat. They were busy, and you're going to be too." With that, he walked out and left Cruz and Carter there, their jaws on the floor.

"Where do you suggest we start?" Carter asked.

"First two. I'll take one, you take the other. Here." Cruz handed Carter a box. Both men produced yellow legal pads from their messenger bags and sat down to work.

An hour later, Cruz finally came up for air. "Whaddya got? Anything noteworthy?"

Carter tossed his pencil onto the table's gleaming surface and tipped backward in his chair. "Not really. Garden variety robbery. Three men, masked, one with a shotgun and the other two with handguns. They throw a bag up in the teller's window and order her to fill it. One's holding the security guard while the other two terrorize the patrons. They get away in a small car parked down the block, and they're long gone before the police arrive. Car's found abandoned later. Stolen. No usable DNA evidence and no leads."

"Same here two months later. Exact same pattern. Same method. Same kind of getaway setup." Cruz sat there for a few seconds, his face smooth as he pondered everything. "I have a feeling the third one is the same. But the fourth one should be the one that will tell us the most."

"Yeah, Sharla called it a 'botched robbery,' whatever that means."

"Want some coffee?"

"Yeah."

"Okay. I'll get us some. Check the last of the reports

on the third one. That should be sufficient. Then we'll dive into the fourth." As Cruz walked out, Carter pulled the last file from the third robbery. Exactly the same. Based on the descriptions, the same man performed the same task each time too, so they had well-defined roles. That was good to know.

"Okay, here we go," Carter said as Cruz returned with the steaming mugs. "You take those and I'll take these." Cruz reached for his pile and they were on it.

Five minutes later, Carter ran across what he was looking for. "This is what I wanted. So here are the accounts of the robbery from the witnesses, and the statements from the officers. See what you make of the officers' accounts and I'll look at the witnesses'," he said, handing Cruz a stack of documents.

Carter skimmed through the witness accounts. They were all pretty much the same, the comments made about actions from different locations' perspectives inside the building, but each confirmed the other. He was getting ready to look through the evidence list when Cruz said, "Whoa! Hold up. I think I just found something."

"Yeah?"

"Here. The officers make statements about the robbery. There are also nine-one-one logs. According to the witnesses, what time did the robbery take place?"

"They all said two thirty-two or thirty-three in the afternoon."

"Well, isn't this interesting? The call to the cops came in at two thirty."

Carter's brow dropped. "Just before the witnesses say it began."

"Yeah. I'm betting nobody noticed that because, you know, watches being off by a few minutes and everything. But what if they're right? What if it was two thirty-two or thirty-three, and that call really did come in a minute or two before the robbery began?"

Carter's brain chattered with questions. "Town this size, response time would be lower than most because of the small geographical area."

"Yeah. So calling it in prior would automatically get law enforcement there by the time it went down. Also says the police officers identified the getaway vehicle because it had been reported stolen twenty minutes before." Cruz sat back in his chair. "Holy shit. These guys were ratted out by somebody. One of them? Hoping the other two would get caught?"

"But they'd all three be caught, and nobody would get the proceeds of the other robberies. Wait—did they ever find the stolen money from the three other robberies?"

Cruz leafed through a stack of papers, then pulled one out. "No. The money was never recovered."

"How much money are we talking about here?"

"Well, the robbery file I looked over was five million."

"The first one was five million also," Carter said, then searched through the stack of papers for the third robbery. "This one was four million."

"Son of a bitch. Fourteen million dollars that was

never recovered." Cruz stood and headed out the door, and Carter wondered where he was going. He was back in three seconds. "Langstaff says none of that money was *ever* recovered. The other two said they had no idea where the third had hidden it."

"Taliq Kent. He kept telling his wife he had an 'insurance policy,' but she never found it. My god. He was the only one who knew where the money was."

"Right. You know what I'm thinking?" Cruz asked.

"Yeah. You're thinking we need to visit those two convicts," Carter said with a nod. "And I'm in agreement."

"You called and they said to come when we wanted, right?"

"Yep. Just give them at least a few hours' notice."

"Well, then, my friend, looks like you and I are going to Pennington Gap, Virginia," Cruz said as he sorted the paperwork and put it back into the boxes. "This should be interesting."

CHAPTER 8

PRISONS ALWAYS CREEPED CARTER OUT, but this one was particularly imposing. It was gray, a whitish gray that blended into the surrounding hills. There was a prison camp on its grounds also, but these two guys weren't in the prison camp. They were definitely in the "big house." The two law enforcement professionals had been told both men would be awaiting their arrival.

To their disappointment, they arrived only to discover that Sean McCutchen was in solitary for attacking a guard and wouldn't be available. *That would've been good information to have*, Carter thought, but they'd made the trip, so they'd work with what they could get. A guard led a shackled prisoner in, a dark-haired man, and guided him to a seat, then locked his cuffs to a ring embedded in the table. As soon as the guard stepped away, Brandon Estevez glared at Carter and Cruz. "What da fuck dis about?"

"I'm Agent Livingston from the FBI's San Antonio

office. This is Sheriff Carter Melton, Trigg County, Kentucky. We're investigating a crime in Sheriff Melton's area and we wanted to talk to you to see if there's a connection between it and your case."

"Whaaa? How dey be a connection? I been here for a while and I don' know nobody in *Kentucky*," he said, almost spitting the state's name as though it was a bitter pill.

"Sir, I'm sure you don't know anything about the particular crime, but it did involve a relative of someone you know. Knew," Cruz corrected. Estevez just glared at him. "Tamara Kent, the daughter of your late friend Taliq."

"Taliq's girl done somethin'? Well, how 'bout dat? What she do?"

"She killed a state trooper," Carter said with as little spite in his voice as he could manage.

"Woo-hooo! No wonder you here to talk to me! I don' know nothin' 'bout dat either."

"No, but you know about the fourteen million dollars." As soon as the words left Cruz's lips, the man's eyes went wide.

"I don' know nothin' 'bout fourteen million dollars, dude. Nope."

"I know, because you have no idea what Taliq did with it, do you?" Carter hiked an eyebrow up as he asked and gave Estevez a smirk.

"No. I don'. And if I did, I wouldn't be tellin' no cop."

"We don't expect you to. But there are some things you could help us with."

"And wha I get outta it?"

"The knowledge that you helped in an ongoing investigation. That should make you feel like Superman," Cruz said, his voice caustic.

"Oh, hahaha. Very funny, lawman. I don' give two shits 'bout no law an' order."

Cruz sat there for a few seconds and Carter wondered what he was going to say. "Well, okay then. What do you do around here?" When Estevez didn't answer, Cruz asked, "Work in the dining hall? Laundry?"

"Bathrooms." *Oh, that's a lovely job*, Carter thought when Estevez answered.

"How 'bout I get you two weeks off bathroom duty?" Cruz asked.

"Make it a month an' we talk."

"Okay. I'll ask for a month. I can't guarantee anything, but I'll ask. Good enough?"

Estevez sat there for a few seconds and Carter was sure he was going to say no when he finally piped up. "Okay. I tell you what you wanna know."

Cruz was primed and ready. "Good. So Kent kept telling his wife he had an insurance policy. Know anything about that? Or was he talking about the money?"

"I guess da money. Dat guy, he don' ever care nothin' 'bout his kids or ol' lady. He was a user, man. Use you up and throw you away. Dat's all he ever do."

"Uh-huh. So if he was calling that his insurance policy, how did he expect them to collect it?"

Estevez shrugged. "He say he had numbers in a book, man. You know, satellite stuff."

"You mean GPS coordinates?" Carter asked, stunned.

"Yeah, man. GPS coordinates. But dat money was for da crew."

"You mean the gang," Cruz corrected.

"I don' like dat word. Sounds so fuckin' negative, ya know." Estevez was grinning as he said it, and Carter wanted to knock that grin right off his face. "But he said we gonna divide it up and be for us, ya know? He say not to tell da Italian, ya know? Because dat dude, he be like wantin' to kill us for it."

"Well, fourteen million dollars *is* a lot of money," Carter pointed out.

"Yeah, but there was more. Dat money, dat not da only thing Kent buried there." The minute the word "buried" popped from Estevez's mouth, it was obvious he'd said something he hadn't meant to.

Carter watched as Cruz leveled his gaze at the prisoner. "Two months off bathroom duty. Spill."

"Well, see, ya know dat ring da Italian wear? He tell Los Lobos, he say he the new leader, dat Don Eduardo turn things over to him an' go underground. But nobody believed him. He say Don Eduardo give him the ring. Dat's not what Kent say."

"And what did Kent say?"

"He say Don Eduardo is dead."

186

Carter and Cruz glanced at each other. "And who killed him?"

"Kent. For da Italian."

Now we're getting somewhere, Carter thought. "So are you saying Eduardo is buried with the money?"

"I think so. I mean, dat make sense, ya know? An' da Italian, he don' want dat body showin' up."

"Because they'll know Don Eduardo is dead and not hiding out?" Carter asked.

"No. Because dey dig up dat body, dey see dat ring finger missing where da Italian cut it off an' take dat ring."

It hit Carter like a ton of bricks. The Italian had Don Eduardo killed to take over Los Lobos, but it hadn't worked the way he'd planned. They were resistant, and they were right to be. If the members of Los Lobos ever found out Don Eduardo was dead and the Italian had taken that ring, the bloodshed would be immediate and never-ending until all the members of *La Tana del Lupo* were dead.

"Does McCutchen know about all of this too?" Cruz asked Estevez, breaking into Carter's thoughts.

"Oh, yeah, but that mofo, he crazy, man. I stay away from him, man. I don' want nothin' to do wif dat boy, knowwhatI'msayin'?"

Cruz nodded along as he spoke. "Well, okay then. And you have no idea where he wrote down the coordinates for the burial site?"

"Nope. But it gotta be somewhere in da stuff wif his wife and kids. No other place it could be."

"And did they know where the wife and kids were?" Carter asked.

"Nope. Dey been lookin' for 'em all dese years, but I hear dey found 'em. Ain't dat funny, boy? I hear dey in *Ken-tu-cky*," he said, emphasizing each syllable in a way that made Carter want to punch him. "Dat girl of Kent's, she got a birthmark on her face. Dey lookin' for her. Say she a college kid. Who ever guess Kent's girl go to *college*?"

The sheriff felt sick. *That's* what *La Tana del Lupo* was doing—looking for those coordinates. They'd been looking for a while, and they'd finally found the kids. So many things were running through Carter's mind that he couldn't speak. He just wanted to get out of the prison and in the car with Cruz so he could voice everything he was thinking to see if he could be right about any of it.

His thoughts were interrupted again by Cruz. "I think we're done here. Thank you for your time, Mr. Estevez. I'm going to the warden right now to talk about your bathroom duty, and I hope I can get that for you."

"You'd better, FBI man. Nothin' in life is free. Don'cha know dat?" Estevez laughed loudly at his own joke and Carter was sickened again. All he could think of in that moment was Sharla, the kids, and getting some fresh air into his lungs. The stale air in the prison interrogation room had become stifling.

As soon as Estevez was led out, Cruz turned to Carter. "You okay?"

"No. No, I'm not. I need to get out of here."

"Okay. Come on. You can wait out front while I go talk to the warden." He let Cruz deposit him at the front doors by the desk, and as soon as Cruz was out of sight, he propped his elbows on his knees and dropped his face into his hands.

"Hey." He looked up to find a young guard standing over him. "You okay?"

"Not at all okay."

"Got some bad news, huh?"

"Yeah." Carter didn't even know how to articulate what he was thinking and feeling.

"This place doesn't help. First two weeks I worked here, I went home sick every day. It's ... a scary place to be."

"I'll say."

"Do you need some water? Or a soft drink?"

"No, no. I'm fine. But thanks for checking on me." Cruz appeared just as the words left Carter's lips, and he stood to go.

They'd no more than closed the car doors when Cruz said, "You're looking a little shaky, bud."

"I *am* a little shaky."

"And I know why. Let's get the hell off the grounds and stop somewhere to talk." Carter started the car, drove to the checkpoint, and cleared the gate. Two miles down the road, he pulled into the parking lot of a dollar-type store and stopped. "Talk to me, Carter."

"God, Sharla and the kids ... This is serious shit. The Italian really believes that somewhere in their home are the coordinates for the burial site. He wants them before anybody else finds them."

"Yeah. That means he's going to be rattling cages and shaking trees."

"Yeah. And they're the trees." Carter ran a hand through his hair in frustration. "What do we do? Put them in protective custody?"

"So far, nobody's hurt either of the kids or Sharla, or even attempted to."

"But Tamara ..."

"Tamara was an unexpected casualty. They didn't want her dead; they wanted to use her."

The sheriff shook his head in disbelief. "But in the meantime, as they looked for her, they poisoned dozens of college campuses with their rhetoric and drugs."

"I think they're probably using kids to move illegal firearms too."

Carter's eyes popped open even wider. "Holy shit. This is ... Cruz, we're going to need some help with all this."

"We can handle it, but we've got something very, very important we've got to do first." When Carter gave him a sideways stare, Cruz pursed his lips and set his jaw before he spoke. "We've got to find those coordinates."

* * *

CRUZ TRIED TO MAKE SMALL TALK ALL THE WAY BACK TO

Kentucky, but Carter knew what he was doing and he was having none of it. He fucking well didn't feel like talking. One thing was certain. If they could find the coordinates, unearth the money and the body, and expose the whole thing, the Italian would be in a shit ton of trouble. But they'd have another problem on their hands—full-blown, all-out gang war between Los Lobos and *La Tana del Lupo*. What was the right choice? Find it all and expose the Italian? Or find it all, but suppress the information about the ring finger? Of course, letting the two gangs fight it out until they killed each other off was an attractive idea, but the collateral damage of civilian casualties would be huge, and they didn't want that.

It was early Sunday morning before they pulled into Carter's drive. Cruz had told him several times that they should stop and stay the night, but he didn't want to. He wanted to keep driving, to get home, to check on Sharla, Chelsea, and Lionel. He'd talked to her and texted her several times, but he didn't dare tell her anything. He also talked to Glen and asked him to keep watching her and to ask the Hopkinsville police chief to do the same. His friend assured him they would. That was the best he could ask for.

They headed off to bed. Carter could hear Cruz snoring even through the wall, but he couldn't close his eyes. His mind was churning, thinking of all the info they'd gained, the crimes that had been committed, and the hatred between the two gangs. He had one small shred of hope. It appeared Estevez knew nothing about

Imogen's death or Sharla taking in Tamara and Lionel, and they certainly hadn't told him. He knew those guys still talked to the outside, and the less the Italian knew about them, the better. It was bad enough that Angelico had found them. He was most certainly the one who was either following Sharla or had someone doing so.

By the next morning, he was a wreck. All he could think about was Sharla, Chelsea, Lionel, and their safety. That was what he really wanted to work on, but Cruz had other ideas. "Get hold of Sharla. We need to start going through her sister's things."

It took a trip to the hospital to pick up a key from Sharla, but by lunchtime, they had the lock off the self-storage unit and were loading boxes in Carter's truck. They weren't hard to spot—they all had Imogen's name on them. There were about twelve of them, and it struck Carter as extremely sad that a life could be reduced to a dozen boxes.

It seemed hopeless. Nothing but random stuff filled the boxes, one box after another. There were a few ribbons and a trophy from high school, four high school yearbooks, and a box of pictures of all kinds. Carter sifted through them in the conference room of the department. There were kids, and he could tell they were Tamara and Lionel. There were also some pics of who he assumed was Imogen with Taliq. If they were wedding pictures, nothing formal had taken place. It looked like they were at a courthouse. Many were pictures of two young girls with an older couple, and as he stared at them, he realized it was Imogen and Sharla with their parents. God, Sharla looked just like her mother! And Imogen looked just like their dad. He thought for a few seconds about his own mom and how he needed to talk to her, to explain why he hadn't introduced Sharla earlier and how it had all come to be, but that would have to wait. Finding what they were searching for, getting to the bottom of the whole thing, was all he had time to do. They *had* to find those coordinates, but it was almost impossible with the wealth of pure junk they were going through.

There were only two more boxes when Carter opened one of them. "Bingo."

"Yeah?"

Carter looked up at Cruz and grinned. "Journals."

"Now I'm getting hopeful," Cruz said and reached in for a handful of them. "Might as well dig in."

The first one was obviously written when Imogen was in middle school. She talked about some boy named David and how cute he was. She bitched about her mom making her clean the kitchen after dinner by herself for a week for talking on the phone when she wasn't supposed to. There was a whole detailed section about how she skipped school by getting on the bus, getting off at school, and slipping away instead of going inside. She threw them off for several days because the school bus driver swore she was on the bus, which she was. Carter had to hand it to her, she was successfully sneaky. But nothing in the journal was anything more than the ramblings of a young girl.

The next one he picked up had a cover decorated

with hearts and flowers, and he dreaded that. Sure enough, it was high school, and it was awful. To his horror, she wrote a detailed account of the night she lost her virginity in the bed of a pickup truck behind the football stadium after the game. She only mentioned the boy by his initials, *QB*, and then he realized—quarterback. She was a pretty girl, so she got one of the popular, important players to look at her. He dug out one of the yearbooks and looked in the back. One inscription caught his eye: *To Imogen, one of the most funnest girls I've ever known. Stay sexy, babe.* He looked at the name and then flipped to the athletic pages. Sure enough, the boy was the quarterback of the high school football team. *Guess my powers of investigation are intact*, he laughed inwardly as he put the yearbook back and went on through the journal. It yielded zip.

The next one he picked up was different. It was blue, a light shade like the rest of them, but there was a difference—there was nothing on the cover. Just plain light blue. He flipped it open and started to read.

June 7 – Taliq and I went to the park today with Tamara, but I wish he hadn't gone. He fussed at her the whole time. When I mentioned it in the car, he slapped me hard. I hope Mom and Dad don't see the finger marks. The journal entry went on in that fashion until Carter was sick of it. He dug farther into it. Nothing. Just the same kinds of things.

Reaching for another one, he opened it and found a much different kind of journal, even though it was pretty and colorful on the outside like the others. Some of the entries were true entries, but some were rambling and incoherent, things he couldn't make any sense out of. On at least a couple of pages were grocery or drugstore lists. Thumbing on through it, he found long periods where the pages were filled with the usual, and then two or three here or there with the weird stuff. It seemed totally random. When he got to the back, he looked at the last entry: March of the year the robbery occurred. Flipping back through it, he saw nothing that gave him pause, so he went back to the end. That was when he saw it.

The bottom of the page almost appeared empty, but there were marks there, very light pencil marks, three lines of horizontal lines and two of vertical. Five in all. There was no pattern that he could discern, and it didn't look to be a binary kind of thing. "Hey, take a look at this."

Cruz crossed the small space and stared at it. "Well, that's odd."

"Yeah. I have no idea what they are. Almost looks like somebody was counting something, but there are no diagonal lines, so that can't be it. Wonder if it's some kind of calendar markings minus the calendar?"

"I suppose that's possible. Got a date on it?"

"Not really. The last date was in March, barely three months before the last robbery, but there was one that month."

"What were the dates on the robberies again? Do you remember?"

"One was in November of the previous year. One in

January. And one in March. If that was intended to be a pattern, looks like they missed a month." Carter thought about it for a minute. "Maybe that's what set Angelico gunning for the guys. Maybe he wanted another robbery in May but they balked."

"Could be. Maybe he was mad at them, and when he asked why they hadn't carried it out, Kent blasted off about having the money from the first three and not needing more?"

That made sense to Carter. "Maybe. Sounds like a good theory. Wish I'd asked Estevez about that."

Cruz shrugged. "Doesn't matter what set Angelico off—something did. Enough to try to get three men killed. I'm guessing if he got them arrested, he was going to promise to get a release for the first one to flip on Kent."

"But they knew nothing."

Cruz nodded. "Exactly."

"I'm not leaving this here. I'm taking it with us." Carter slipped the journal into his messenger bag and headed out of the office, Cruz right behind him. "I'm pretty sure this is what we're looking for. Now to see if anybody can figure it out."

* * *

"OUR CODE BREAKERS THINK IT'S A BINARY CODE OF some sort, but we can't figure out what. It doesn't make sense." The voice of James Maddux, San Antonio FBI office's chief analyst, came rolling out of the phone.

"But we're still working on it. We've put it into several translation devices, but so far, nothing."

"Okay. Thanks. We appreciate it. Let me know if you crack it."

"Will do."

"And that's that," Cruz said, reaching for the phone and turning off the speaker.

"At least they're working on it." Carter was frustrated. They'd had the journal for two days and nobody had been able to figure it out. He'd stared at it for hours himself, but nothing had come to him.

Cruz grabbed his jacket. "I'm having dinner with Sam and Dahlia. Wanna come along?"

Carter shook his head. "Thanks, but nah. I'm betting when I get home, Sharla's there."

"Want me to stay with them tonight so you guys have the run of the house?" Cruz asked, grinning.

"No need. I'll probably come back here."

"No! You should get some rest! We've been working night and day on this. Take a break. It'll come together. Our analysts are the best. They'll get it."

"But what if they don't?"

Cruz rolled his eyes. "Okay then. You want to sit here and stare at that paper all night, you go right ahead. I'm getting some rest. Catch up with you later." With a backhanded wave, he was gone.

Carter stood and stretched, then grabbed his own jacket and headed to the house. Sure enough, Sharla's car was in the driveway. "Something smells good in here!" he called out as he opened the door.

"Good! I didn't burn it too badly!" she yelled back, laughing. When he stepped into the kitchen, she met him with a smile and a big wooden spoon in her hand. "Hi!"

"Hi." The kiss she gave him was a welcome bit of paradise in an otherwise shitty world. "Have a good day?"

"Good enough. You?"

"Still haven't had any movement in that development." He hadn't told her what they were working on, so if anyone asked, she honestly didn't know. That was best for her safety.

"Bummer. Maybe you'll get a break tomorrow. How does spaghetti sound?"

"If it tastes as good as it smells, it'll be delicious." *How ironic—I'm eating Italian food while an Italian is terrorizing my world*, his brain muttered and he almost laughed. "Back in a minute."

Changing into a pair of jeans and a tee, Carter looked in the mirror and finger-combed his hair. When he padded sock-footed back into the kitchen, Sharla had plates on the table and was pulling hot bread from the oven. "You really went to a lot of trouble. Anything I can do to help?"

"Yeah. Get some dressing out of the refrigerator. I want Italian, of course. Get whatever you like too. Oh, and the grated parmesan."

Italian sounded good to him, so he pulled the bottle from the refrigerator's door and grabbed the can of cheese. She'd already placed the salad plates on the table, and the salad was green and leafy and looked delicious. "Wow. This looks … wow. Babe, you didn't have to—"

"I know, but I was hungry for spaghetti and I like to have a salad with it. And nobody—*nobody*—cooks spaghetti for just themselves. If you're going to do it, there have to be leftovers."

"Won't be any tonight. I plan to eat every bite," Carter announced as he sat down and placed the dressing and cheese on the table.

But he didn't. There was way too much, and he realized she'd made enough for Cruz in anticipation of him being there. She hadn't asked where he was, but he knew she wondered, so he told her. He got a frown in return. "Pity. I wanted to get to know him a little better."

"Oh, Chelsea's 'mom, get to know that good-looking guy' routine get to you after all?" he asked and grinned.

"No. He just seems … interesting. He has somebody, right?"

"Yeah. Her name's Mickie and from what I can tell, the guy's totally smitten."

"That's sweet. I don't know anybody else who's totally smitten with somebody except me."

"Hey, wait a minute!" Carter cried in mock argument. "I'm totally smitten with you!"

"Oh, you are?"

"Yeah. I am. But you already know that."

"So what are we doing tonight? Watching some of

that sitcom on streaming? Going to the grocery? Rolling around in your bed for a few hours?" she asked and winked.

He knew she was going to have a fit. "No. I'm going back to the office."

"Carter! What the hell? You've been there for two days, and you've barely taken a break! Can't it wait until tomorrow?"

How could he explain to her that in one blinding second, he could unravel the puzzle and all the pieces would fall into place? "Babe, there's so much paperwork with this case that if I don't stay on top of it, it'll get out of hand. But it'll be over soon, I promise."

"But I miss you," Sharla whined. That kind of whining was very unlike her, and he wondered if he was pushing his luck.

"I know. I miss you too. But we're too close to solving this to just walk away. I'll figure it out."

"How long is that going to take?"

Carter sighed. "I don't know. I'm surprised it hasn't happened yet. It's got to be pretty simple, and yet I don't know what it is."

"Carter?"

"Hmm?"

"Do you love me?"

"Yes. I do. With all my heart." He'd never said that before, and it felt good.

"Good. Because I love you with all my heart, and I'd hate to think I'm wasting my time."

"You are not wasting your time, girl. It's just that

you and the kids … you're my priority. My job is to keep you safe, to make sure you're protected and sheltered, to make sure your lives are as good as they can be. This is just a little bump in the road, sweetie. Nothing more."

Sharla sighed loudly and slumped in her chair. "Well, okay. Whatever. Do what you have to do."

Carter had heard that before, and it was time to find out exactly where he stood. "My ex-girlfriend used to say that shit to me too. Are we going to do this for several years until you finally just walk out one day?" He hoped his stare was piercing enough to let her know he wanted her to think about her answer.

But she didn't. She didn't even hesitate. "Nope. I'm here for the duration, Carter Melton. I don't give a shit if you don't come home for three days. As long as I know you're not in bed with Penny Tadlock, it'll be—"

"Who told you about—"

"You did, silly. Remember?"

"Oh … yeah. Well, then, you should know that she's the Methodist minister's ex-wife, and I'm not interested in *that* at all."

She laughed aloud. "What, you don't like a bit of a scandal?"

"Nope. Don't need that mess at all." He grinned. "No re-election for me if that happens."

"I guess not." She sat silent for a little while before she looked up and into his eyes. "Carter, I love you. Do whatever you think you have to do. I'll still be here."

Reaching across the table, he took her hand and

squeezed it. "Thank you. I love you, and that means everything to me."

"So how long are you staying?"

"I'll leave in about twenty minutes, but I really think I need to call my mom and talk to her for a few minutes."

"That's a good son," she said with a grin. "You do that."

As soon as the phone call was over, during which he managed to deflect almost every question Wilda Fern asked, he kissed Sharla goodbye and headed back to the office. Lewis and Edwards were on patrol that evening. He liked it when he could arrange it that way, Lewis being his senior deputy and Edwards being the rookie. If Mike had a question, Gray could most certainly answer it. He'd only been there for about fifteen minutes when the door opened and Edwards strode in. "Sheriff! What are you doing here?"

"Going over stuff in this case." Carter slapped his hands together, then opened them and rubbed them down his face before dropping them to his lap. "And I think it's about to whup me. What are you doing?"

"Found this." Edwards held up a backpack that had obviously seen better days. "It was lying near a dumpster, but it's got some jewelry and electronics in it. I'd say somebody got robbed and doesn't know it yet."

"Sounds like it. Log it in and if they come looking, we can get their particulars." He stared at the rows of marks again. God, he wished he could piece that mystery together and solve it.

"Yes, sir."

Concentrating on the markings, he didn't hear Edwards come up behind him until he sensed the deputy there. "Shit!" Carter yelled and jumped. "You scared the hell out of me! What are you doing?"

"Looking over your shoulder," Edwards said with a grin. "What is that?"

He started to rail at the young man, then thought about it for a split second. *What could it hurt to show him?* "It's some kind of clue or message or something. We found it in connection to a crime, and we're trying to figure it out."

"Huh." He could practically see the gears turning in Mike's mind. "Got a ruler?"

"Yeah." Carter dug around in his desk drawer and produced one.

"Mind if I sit down with this for a minute?"

"Don't make any marks on those pages!"

"I won't, sir. I would never do that. I just want to check something." Reluctantly, Carter handed off the journal and the ruler, and Mike sat down at another desk with it. In a few minutes, he stood and headed to the copy machine.

"What are you doing?"

"Hang on, sir. I think I'm on to something here." He watched as Mike made several copies of the page, then took them back. Carter tried to busy himself with something else, but curiosity was getting the better of him. "Scissors, sir?"

"Sure." *Okay, this is ridiculous*, Carter thought, but he

handed Edwards the scissors and sat back down. The young deputy cut the copies into strips and began to arrange them oddly. "What exactly are you doing?"

"I think I figured it out, sir."

No fucking way! Carter wanted to yell. "Oh, you do, do you?"

"Yeah. Come look."

Carter watched as Edwards drew a line on a plain sheet of paper. Each strip he'd cut had two horizontal lines on it that bordered the marks there. He put the plain paper on top of a strip, lined up the lines on the paper with the lines on the strips, and traced the markings on the strip. When he finished the first one, he moved on to the second strip, doing the exact same thing.

Carter's mouth flew open. They were digital numbers, the kind seen on an LED clock or a gas pump. As Edwards traced each strip in turn, they became clearer and clearer as they went from their original chaos into complete organization.

"There you go, sir. Does this mean anything to you?" Edwards said and handed the paper to Carter.

They were strings of number, but he recognized them immediately, held them up, and turned back to Edwards. "What do you see, deputy?" he asked, praying Edwards confirmed his thoughts.

"Looks like GPS coordinates to me, sir."

Carter couldn't believe it. The twenty-four-year-old rookie had solved a puzzle that he and Cruz had been looking at for days. Not only that, FBI analysts were working on it with no luck. They'd all tried to turn it into its own language and make it harder than it had to be, but it was simple—*too* simple. "Well, I'll be damned. Mike, I owe you a steak dinner."

"Thank you, sir!" the young man chirped, beaming. "Glad I could help!"

"You earned it. And say nothing, do you hear me? Nothing to *anybody*."

"Yes, sir. Got it, sir. Nothing to anybody. My lips are sealed."

Carter took the paper and looked at it, then opened his laptop and started typing. For some reason, it crossed his mind to use a proxy server, so he found a free one and typed in the information. There were several different formats for latitude and longitude coordinates, and he needed to figure out which one was correct. Ten numbers—decimal degrees, but without the decimals. They would go after the first two numbers in each five-number string. No letters, but he knew north came first and then west. If they made no sense when he looked them up that way, he'd reverse them on the outside chance that Taliq had done the same. He found a site on which to enter them, took a deep breath, and waited.

And he almost fell out of his chair. The site was about five blocks from the courthouse in O'Fallon, right where they'd been just days before. Then he typed them into a map of aerial photography and waited. What the hell was that? It was weird looking, that was for sure. He zoomed in as closely as he could and stared at it. That weird object ...

It was a scrap yard. The odd things he was seeing all around? Crushed cars. And the object in the center? A crane. Taliq had buried the money and the body in plain sight, and no one had ever detected it. Matter of fact, if the picture was accurate, it was dead in the middle of the drive that ran straight through the yard. How had he buried it there and nobody noticed? Had there been a connection between Taliq and the scrap yard? Carter could ask Sharla, but he didn't think she'd know. She seemed to have little knowledge of her sister's life until Imogen moved back due to her illness.

But there was a bigger question. Who was he going to tell? Nobody. As he thought about it, he decided he had to tell Cruz, but that was it. No one else. Until they could figure out how to lure Cabo Paolo and his henchmen to the site and arrest them, Cruz was to say nothing to anyone. Not one word. There was more at stake than just his reputation. He had to think about Sharla, Chelsea, and Lionel's safety, and if that information got out, they wouldn't be safe. No one could know.

No one.

CHAPTER 9

MORNING CAME TOO SOON. He said goodbye to Sharla as she left for work and then headed back into the kitchen. Ten minutes later, Cruz wandered in and got a cup of coffee. Twenty minutes later, he knew everything Carter knew.

"Why the hell didn't you call me and tell me?" Cruz almost screamed. "My god! You broke the code and—"

"I didn't break the code. Edwards did."

"So he knows?"

"I told him to keep his mouth shut, and he will."

"I hope you're right." Cruz sat there for a few seconds, deep in contemplation, and Carter wanted to dance. His own deputy, a wet-behind-the-ears rookie, had figured out what everyone else had struggled with. It was true—sometimes a fresh perspective was all that was needed.

"I suppose I should call the analysts and—"

"No!"

"Yes. I don't want government funds wasted when we've figured it out."

"Then tell them we determined they were meaningless scribbles."

Cruz frowned. "You know they're not going to buy that."

"Try. I'd rather they—"

The ringing of Cruz's phone interrupted Carter's sentence. "Hang on. This is my boss in San Antonio." Carter watched as Cruz hit the button to accept the call. "Livingston. Hey, yeah, still here. We … What? Yeah, the other day." Cruz's frown deepened and Carter wondered what was up. "But he was in solitary. Uh-huh. Yeah." Something was going on, and Carter wanted to know what it was. "Oh, how coincidental, huh? Yeah. Let me know. Sure. Thanks." Cruz hit end and stared at Carter. "You're not going to believe this."

"Try me."

"The prison had my contact info, so they called the office. Estevez and McCutchen?" Carter nodded. "Dead."

Carter was sure he'd heard wrong. "What?"

"They're dead. Estevez was involved in a fight in the dining room and knifed in the stomach by another inmate."

"But McCutchen was in solitary."

"Yeah. Hanged himself from the bars in the window with a bedsheet."

Carter could feel his eyebrows shoot up. "You don't believe any of that, do you?"

"Not for a minute. I think we need to go back to that self-storage facility and pull everything that belonged to Imogen, bring it to your office, and lock it down."

"Let's go." Carter ran to the bedroom, dragged on a pair of jeans and a tee, and met Cruz back at the front door.

And when they drove up in front of the building, Carter's heart froze. The door was wide open and things were strewn everywhere, boxes overturned and items broken and dashed against the walls. "Holy fuck."

"I think the holy fuck is that we're here between a bunch of aluminum buildings where no one on the street can see us. We're sitting ducks. Get us the hell out of here," Cruz hissed, and Carter threw the truck into gear and tore out between the buildings and back onto the street. As soon as the truck was a block down the street, Carter heard Cruz sigh before he asked, "Why do I get the feeling we were being watched?"

"Because I'm pretty sure we were. And if they know that journal was in Sharla's building and it's not there anymore, they're watching her too. My god. What do we do?"

"We make sure she's safe and then check on the kids. There's little else we can do."

"You could assign agents to her and the kids! We could take them to a safehouse! We've got to do *something*!" Carter screamed at Cruz.

"But they'll be the ones who flush *La Tana del Lupo*

out. They'll come looking for that information. When they do, we'll be ready."

"I don't like this. I don't want people I love used as bait." And it was true—he cared about Chelsea and Lionel because Sharla loved them. Tamara had already been used as a pawn. What else would these men do?

"I'm calling my superiors. We need some help down here, Carter. I know you didn't want anybody else to—"

"Call them! Call the fucking National Guard! Call anybody you can! I want them safe, understand? *I want them SAFE!*"

Carter watched as Cruz flipped through the contacts on his phone and placed a call, but he had to leave a message. Fuck it all. Leaving a message wasn't good enough. Carter needed to do something, but he didn't know what. Sharla was in danger and she had no idea. He had to tell her. And he had to keep her safe.

There was no other option.

* * *

"What? What are you saying? All of this was about Taliq?" Sharla's eyes were almost popping out and her jaw dropped.

"No. It's about fourteen million dollars and a dead guy, Sharla. A very important dead guy, at least in the gangland world. And fourteen million dollars. A lot of people would kill for fourteen million dollars." Carter's hands were shaking as he tried to explain to her. He knew he was repeating himself, but it didn't matter.

"What am I supposed to do?"

"Stay here. At the hospital. As long as you stay here and we alert security, you'll be safe."

"What about the kids? They're at school."

"Not for long, they're not," Cruz answered before Carter could.

"Sam's already headed that direction to check on them. He should—" Carter's phone rang and he looked down: Sam. "Yeah?"

"They're fine. We're leaving a pair of plainclothes with them. When are the rest of those FBI guys coming?"

"I have no idea, but I hope it's soon." Carter was bouncing his heel on the floor as he spoke. He couldn't help it. It was as though his whole life was coming unraveled and he was powerless to do anything about it.

"Okay. Well, our guys will keep an eye on them, but we need to get them out of here. This place is the worst place in the whole world that they could be."

"I agree. Campuses are impossible to lock down. Keep in touch with me and your guys out there. And thanks, Sam."

"Sure thing. We're on it." The phone went dead.

"That was Sam. The kids are fine and they've got guys watching them." He thought Sharla would breathe a sigh of relief, but she didn't.

"Agents are coming in from Louisville and

Lexington as we speak," Cruz said, looking at the screen of his phone. "Just got the text."

"Okay. You stay here. Don't leave for any reason, do you hear me?" He squeezed Sharla's hand. "You're in the middle of a hospital full of people. You'll be fine."

"But the kids—"

"They'll be fine. We're handling it. I've got to go. I'll talk to you in a little bit, okay?" Carter kissed her forehead before turning to the door. "We need to go. We've got things to do."

"Yeah, things to do," Cruz echoed, and Carter could tell he was wondering what those things were. *Oh, buddy, if only you knew*, Carter told himself as they went. "Where are we going?"

"We're going to my office. There are some things we need to go through." *God will forgive me for lying just this once*, Carter thought as they rolled that direction. As soon as they cleared the office door, he looked around and knew it had worked out just as he wanted it to—Edwards was the only other deputy there. "Cruz, can you go to the conference room and find that evidence list? From the robberies?"

"Uh, sure. No problem. Hang on."

As soon as he disappeared, Carter wheeled on Edwards. "Do you remember those coordinates?"

"No, sir."

"Good." Carter pulled the journal from his desk drawer and ripped the page with the markings out of the back. Then he dug through the trash can until he found the strips of paper and Edwards' work. Lastly, he went to his computer and deleted his cookies and history. That left them unable to trace the proxy server. If they wanted that information, they'd have to work for it.

Stepping outside the front door, Carter stared at the paper. He'd always had an uncanny ability to remember numbers, and these were no exception, especially since lives depended on it. Then he pulled a book of matches he'd found in his desk drawer out of his pocket, struck one, and stood there on the sidewalk, burning the papers. *I hope you motherfuckers see me doing this!* Carter wanted to yell. *I hope you know I'm your only hope, and you'll have to come through me to get to them!* There was a sound behind him and he heard Cruz yell, "What the hell are you doing?"

Carter spun on him. "Me. I'm the only one who has the coordinates now. They want them, they'll have to come to me. They can leave Sharla and the kids alone, because they can't do anything for those bastards. It's me and only me."

"Carter, what have you done? You might as well have a bull's eye on your back!" Cruz barked.

"Let them come. They hurt those kids, Sharla, or me, and they'll NEVER get those coordinates. Never. And I have no intention of giving them up anyway."

"They'll torture you until you give them what they want."

"Then let them come." *Let them come*, Carter told himself again. He wasn't afraid. He'd told that women he'd keep her and those kids safe, and he'd just insured it.

"Jesus Christ!" Cruz yelled from behind him and threw the office door open so hard that it banged against the brick. Oddly, Carter felt a strange measure of peace. He'd done what he had to do. When he stepped inside, Cruz was on the phone. "This idiot just set himself up to get killed! What's the ETA on those agents? Dear god. Okay then. We'll be waiting like fish in a barrel."

"What's going on?" Edwards asked, blinking rapidly.

"Nothing. Go home. Or go out on patrol. But stay away from the office," Carter ordered.

"But, sheriff—"

"GO!" Carter bellowed, and the young officer grabbed his belt and his jacket and high-tailed it from the office.

Cruz wheeled on him and glared. "Do you realize what you've done?"

"Yes. I'm leading you guys straight to them."

"But you'll be the sacrificial lamb. If we swoop down on them and you're with them, they'll kill you on the spot and won't think twice."

"But Sharla and the kids will be safe."

"But without you! Fuck, Carter, there were so many other ways this could've gone! We could've played it dozens of ways that would've been safer for you!"

"But not for them."

Cruz sat down hard on the edge of the desk and

sighed. "I hope you don't have anything you've left undone, because I don't think you've got much time left."

The office grew silent, and Carter sat down behind his desk. So many things he wanted to do ... He'd done a lot with his dad before the elder Melton had died, but after his father's death, Carter had started to make his own bucket list. It was pretty short too, not to mention simple. *Stay on an isolated tropical island. Sit in front of the fire in a lodge in the Rockies. Throw out the ball at the opening of baseball season for one of the big teams.* Those were the only ones he could think of. Well, there was one more.

Dance all night with the woman I love in my arms.

He'd thought that one had no chance of ever happening, and of all of them, that was the one that might've actually happened. Now it never would. Cruz was right, and he knew it—as soon as *La Tana del Lupo* had the information they needed, they'd kill him. But that was okay. Sharla and the kids would be safe.

That would just have to be enough.

"YEAH. OKAY. SEE YOU THEN." CRUZ TURNED TO Carter, who was sitting at his desk, linking paper clips together mindlessly. "They're about three hours out. They just got the team completely assembled. Bad news. The guys from Lexington aren't coming. But they're sending some from Cincinnati, although they probably won't get here in time."

"Um-hmm." Carter didn't even look. Why should he? It was just a matter of time.

Cruz pulled up a chair in front of his desk and leaned in. "Buddy, give me the coordinates too. At least two of us will have them, and that will buy you some safety."

Carter shook his head decisively. "No. No way am I endangering anybody else."

Dropping back in his chair, Cruz let out a sigh Carter was sure was pure irritation. "You are the most determined son of a bitch I've ever seen."

"Yep." His phone rang and he glanced at the screen. Sam. "Yeah?"

"We've got a problem."

Carter sat straight up in his chair. "What? What's happened?"

"I can't locate my guys at the school. They're not responding by radio or phone."

Carter was already grabbing his coat. "We're on the way. You hear me? We'll be there as fast as we can. Let me know if you find them."

"What? What's going on?" Cruz demanded.

"The guys watching the kids. Radio silence. Nobody's seen them." He needn't have asked Cruz to come. The tall Texan was right on his ass all the way to the cruiser.

Lights flashing and siren blaring, Carter drove like a maniac through Cadiz and kept going at over one hundred miles an hour. He whizzed past one state resort park, through Canton, flew over the bridge there, and tore into the Land Between the Lakes National Recreation Area. As soon as he crossed the bridge over Kentucky Lake, Highway 68 turned, but he headed straight in on Highway 80 toward Murray, his tires barely touching the pavement. He glanced briefly over at Cruz, but the agent showed no signs of fear or anger, so he kept going. There was no choice but to slow down when he reached the junction of 80 and 641, but he made the turn on a green light and floored the cruiser for the end of the trip to the school.

Pulling up close to the faculty building, he was stunned. There were cruisers everywhere, officers everywhere, and ... an ambulance. "Oh, shit. We're too late," he whispered.

"Let's go." Cruz was already out of the car and running by the time Carter closed his door.

The first person they recognized was Sam. "The kids!" Carter screamed.

"They're fine, they're fine. Two FBI agents from Louisville just took them to a safehouse. They're okay."

"Then the bus ..." Carter began, pointing to the ambulance.

"Two dead officers. Found them in a breezeway between two buildings."

Carter felt sick. "Shit. Shit, shit, shit. How long ago?"

"It appears it was just about the time I called you and told you we couldn't reach them. I got nervous and decided that—" Sam stopped and turned toward one of the officers who stood beside a cruiser. "What was that transmission?"

"Shots fired at Christian County Community Hospital. Two security officers wounded and a nurse as well." Carter could feel the blood draining from his face as the officer keyed the mic. "Christian County dispatch, this is Murray City unit seven. Could you repeat that transmission, over?"

"Murray City unit seven, this is Christian County dispatch. Shots fired at Christian County Community Hospital. Two security officers wounded, one hospital personnel wounded. Two men, average height, in masks. Hostage taken. Repeat, hostage taken. Subject left the area in a ..."

"Son of a bitch," Carter mumbled. They had Sharla. He'd promised her he'd protect her and the kids, he'd be their shelter and refuge, and he'd fucked everything up. The odds were that even if he helped them, gave them the info they wanted, they'd kill her. *What do I do?* he asked himself over and over. "It's me they want. It's me. If they'll just—" His phone rang and Carter stared at the screen. It was a number he'd never seen before, and he knew what life he had left was about to change forever when he answered it. "Yeah?"

"Sheriff Melton?"

"Yes."

"You know who this is."

"I do." Carter glanced around—he had Cruz and Sam's full attention. "Where's Sharla?"

"Where's our information?"

"I have it."

"Then give it to me."

"Oh, no. You'll have to turn her loose and then I'll gladly give it to you."

"Who else has it?"

"Nobody. Nobody but me. It's in my head. I memorized it. No one else knows it."

"And you're sure about this?"

"Yes. I'm positive. I don't want anybody else getting hurt. Take me, but turn her loose."

"How do I know you won't double-cross me?"

"Because I love her and I'd *never* do anything to jeopardize her safety—never."

"You already have, idiot. If you can't deliver the info to me, she's dead."

"You kill her and you'll *never* get it, do you understand? I have to *know* proof-positive that she's fine or you get nothing. Absolutely nothing."

"You drive a hard bargain for a man with very few hours left in his life."

"I do. So what do I have to lose? Nothing. You let her go and the info is yours."

"You will come home. You will come alone. You will tell no one where you're going. And you will be here within the hour."

"I will."

"Good. I'll let her live at least that long. The clock's ticking, pig. Get on it." With that, the phone went dead.

"Carter, don't do this," Cruz pleaded. "Please, don't. Let us—"

"What? Grovel and posture until he kills her? No. This has to happen." He turned and headed for the cruiser.

"Carter! Wait!" He stopped and turned as Cruz ran up to him. "Would you please do me one favor? Why? Tell me why? Why are you doing this? Just throwing your life away?"

How could he explain? There was only one way he could think of. "All my life, there've been things I should've done, I could've done, and I didn't. I've spent my life saying 'if only.' Over and over. 'If only I'd called him one more time. If only I'd just stayed home with her on Christmas Eve. If only I'd fixed that before she fell. If only, if only' … I can't do that anymore, Cruz. I can't face a tomorrow saying to myself, 'If only I'd done what needed to be done, Sharla would be alive. The kids would be fine. Their lives would be intact.' This is it, Cruz, where the rubber meets the road. It's been good knowing you, buddy. Thanks for being here. I've gotta go." Carter ran to the cruiser, then turned back and yelled, "DON'T FOLLOW ME!"

He tore out and headed back to Cadiz. They were waiting for him, and he couldn't let Sharla down.

* * *

HE STOPPED AT THE FIRST DRUGSTORE HE SAW AND picked up a bottle of pain reliever capsules plus a roll of clear packing tape, then opened the bottle and peeled away the seal. After tearing off a couple of pieces of tape, he dumped out a few of the capsules, wrapped them in the tape, trimmed it away with his pocket knife, and put them in his pocket. The idea had come to him as he was leaving the college, and he thought it just might work, at least long enough to get her out of there.

The drive to Cadiz from Murray had never seemed long, but at the moment, it seemed to stretch into eternity. What would he find when he got there? He thought about the capsules in his pocket and he knew he'd have to make the announcement early on. Otherwise, it wouldn't work.

Darkness enveloped the house when he pulled up, and he immediately noticed something strange, and a growl escaped his throat. His truck had been moved. The sons of bitches had stolen his own truck and used it to go to the hospital to grab Sharla. Wonder what she thought when she saw that? He figured she thought he was already dead. That was okay. If she thought he was dead, she'd been compliant, and that was what he needed, for her to behave.

He parked the cruiser but left the keys in the ignition. She'd need a way to get out of there, and that would have to do. Taking off his belt, he placed it on the hood, holster on it and gun still in its leather. Right there in full view, he knelt and removed the little twenty-five millimeter Tanfoglio pistol he kept in an ankle holster. They could see what he was doing, he was sure. He laid it on the hood too, holster and all, and lifted his arms. As soon as he got near the house, he reached in his pocket and pulled out one of the capsules, then placed it in his cheek and prayed the tape held. There was no sound or movement when Carter yelled, "Let her go."

The front door opened slowly and a face appeared. "We don't take orders from you, cop. Get your ass up here." Carter walked slowly toward the house, taking the steps one at a time, but when he reached the porch, he stopped. "Well? You gettin' in here or not?"

He moved the capsule around until he held it between his teeth. As soon as he knew the man had seen it, he shoved it back into his cheek. "Thought you should see that."

"What the fuck?"

"Cyanide. You hit me, knock me down, do anything that might cause me to rupture it, and I'm dead. The information dies with me. Understand?"

"We shoot you and it won't matter."

"Yeah, but you still won't have the information." He could see from the look on the guy's face that he had the upper hand in that instance.

"We'll kill her," the greaseball announced.

"You do and I'll bite down into it immediately. I don't want to live without her. So that's your choice. Choose wisely."

"You a smart-ass son of a bitch, know that? Hey, bring her out here!" the man called into the house. Carter could hear voices, and one was a woman's.

"Let me go, you stinky, greasy, jacked-up piece of shit!" it yelled. Yep—that was Sharla. As soon as they shoved her out the door, she screamed, "Carter!" and tried to run toward him, but one of the men held her.

"Hey, babe. I left the keys in the car. Just drive it to the station. Cruz will meet you there. It'll be okay, I promise."

"But the kids! They have them!"

"No. They don't. They killed the two officers watching them to lure us to Murray so they could grab you, but Chelsea and Lionel are fine. The FBI has two agents with them right now."

She turned and glared at the taller man. "You son of a bitch! You told me you had them!" With no hesitation, she spat right in his face and he slapped her—hard.

"Don't hit her!" Carter screamed.

"Bitch had it coming," the guy growled as he wiped his face. "You best go get in that car before we change our minds."

"No! Carter, I'm staying here with you!"

"No. Go, Sharla. Go right now. Please. I beg you. Just go."

"I can't. I can't leave you here with, with, with *them*," she said, her voice full of molten contempt.

"You have to. There's no other way. Go and go now. To the station. Find Cruz. He should be there. He'll be waiting for you, or Sam. Somebody will be there. Go on." When she started to cry, his heart broke, but he shrugged it off. "Do as I say! Do it, Sharla!"

"Okay, okay! Please, don't make me leave you, Carter! Please, I'll—"

"Now, Sharla!" Carter bellowed. "Go!" He waited, his back to the drive, as she walked past him, tears streaming down her face. Creaking sounds filled the air as the car door opened and closed. He heard the cruiser's engine start, and the sound of his weapons sliding across the hood and dropping onto the ground as she backed out of the driveway made his skin crawl. In no time, she drove away and the roar of the Crown Vic's engine dwindled into the distance. As soon as he knew she was out of sight, he cocked an eyebrow. "Okay, so what now?"

"Now you're going to take us to the place where we find what's ours. No tricks. No funny business. No driving us around in circles for the rest of the night. Do you understand?"

"Yeah." The gap-toothed henchman held up a small GPS unit, but Carter shook his head. "Nope. I'm not giving them to you, but I'll take you there." One of the men raised his weapon, but Carter grinned. "You shoot me, you got nothing."

"Shoot you in the leg."

"I'll bite down on this capsule and I'll be gone before you can blink."

From the inside of the house came the sound of boots, heavy boots, and a man appeared in the doorway. "Why don't we just admit that he's got the upper hand, you idiots? Sheriff Melton, I presume?"

"Paolo Angelico."

"I see my reputation has preceded me! Good! So you want to go with us, eh? I think that will be permissible. We can take your truck, no?"

"Sure. Why not? Might as well." *I won't be needing it anyway*, Carter told himself.

"Everybody in." The crew cab wasn't very big, and seven guys didn't fit well. As they rolled down the road, Angelico asked without looking at Carter, "Will we need shovels?"

"From what I could tell, yes. You will."

"Pull in up here at the big discount store and buy a couple of shovels, guys." As soon as they were in the parking lot, two of them hopped out. They were only gone a few minutes before they returned and threw five spades into the back of the truck. As soon as they were back in, Angelico asked, "So, where are we going?"

"O'Fallon, Missouri."

"You know the way to get there from here?" Before Carter could answer, the gang leader added, "Oh, of course you do. That's how you found out about the money. What a shame about them. They were good guys once upon a time."

I knew it. He had them killed, Carter's brain hummed. They rode along in silence except for the times when Carter told them where to turn or which exit to take. When they passed through Cairo, Illinois, they stopped at the only gas station around and got out for a bathroom break, then back into the truck and on the road again.

When they hit the O'Fallon city limits, Carter began to think about what was left. His mother would make sure he was buried—*if* they found his body. It wouldn't be long and he'd get to see his dad again. And his grandparents! He'd never been religious, but he believed people were reunited with their loved ones when they died, and at least that was something to look forward to.

He directed them to turn here and there until the scrap yard loomed in front of them. His guess had been right. It looked like the place had been closed down for at least fifteen years, maybe more, and he was a little surprised that the city hadn't forced the owner to get rid of the stuff. "This is it."

"Needle in a haystack," Angelico mumbled.

Carter shook his head. "No. I know exactly where it is. Well, within twenty-five feet."

"Twenty-five feet?"

"GPS coordinates aren't *that* accurate. It could take a while to dig around the location and find it, but it's there."

"Show me," Angelico said, prodding Carter to get out of the truck.

It was silent there, and the veteran officer couldn't help but think how like a graveyard it was. Every one of those cars had been new at one time. They'd been somebody's pride and joy, just like a child. But as time went by, they lost their shine. Their systems started to break down. At some point, it wasn't worth fixing them anymore. After working as many accidents as he had, he also knew that a great many people had died in some of the vehicles left sitting right there in that scrap yard. Inside many of them bloody, battered bodies, the life gone from them, had rested until some underpaid, overworked EMT or fire department first responder had cut them from the vehicle and taken them to the morgue. It was a graveyard, a huge graveyard, and he was going to die there. Of that he was certain. He thought about the aerial view, what it had looked like. As soon as he passed the crane, still sitting there like a frozen sentinel, he stomped around a little. "Right here."

"You sure?"

"No, I'm not sure it's this exact spot, but it's close enough that if you made a circle around me, it would be within that circle."

"How big of a circle?"

"Move out a little." The men started stepping back, three of them with guns trained on him. When they'd gone far enough, Carter said, "There! It's within this circle somewhere."

"You two and you two—get the shovels and start digging. Give Deputy Dawg here a shovel and let him get to work too. Dig, sheriff. Dig like your life depends on it, because it does." Carter took the shovel that was handed to him and stuck the tip in the ground, tonguing the capsule in his cheek. "Well? Fucking dig!" Angelico yelled, and all five men started working.

It didn't take long before Carter was tired, but he tried to think about Sharla and the kids. Once these guys got what they wanted, they'd leave her and the kids alone. Yeah, they wouldn't have him, but that was okay. He thought Lionel wasn't really very fond of him anyway, and he chuckled. "What's so funny, copper?" one of the guys asked.

"Nothing. Just thinking about something somebody said to me one time. That's all."

Angelico rolled his eyes. "You could spit that capsule out if you want."

"Not a chance." Carter went back to work digging. The ground was packed and it was slow going.

They'd managed to dig five holes deep enough to stand in when Carter's shovel blade hit something solid. He hit it a couple more times and it made a clanging sound. "Found something."

"Keep digging. You," Angelico barked at one of the other guys, "get over here and help him."

"Yes, Capo Paolo," the man answered and jumped into the hole with Carter.

"I'd say we should dig around the edges here," Carter said, shoveling a little more away from whatever it was. As they dug, it became obvious that it was some kind of metal sheet, maybe steel, and it was painted dark blue. Carter gave it a hard stomp. "Hollow. There's something inside there, I'm betting."

"Good going. We'll let you live until the lid comes off and you can see what you've died for," Angelico said, not a shred of humor in his voice. The men continued to dig, and Carter knew his time was dwindling. He tried to picture Sharla in the morning, sleeping peacefully in his bed, her hair fanned out over the pillow, a languid smile on her face and one breast uncovered. It made him smile, thinking of her softness, her warmth, the dampness between her legs when he teased her, the puckering of her nipples when he sucked them. God, she was all he'd ever wanted, and she had to come along at the very end. That was just his luck.

"Got an edge here!" one of the other guys called out.

Angelico clapped his hands. "Good. Dig along it and let's see if we can get that thing open." They shoveled a little more out. "Clean it up, guys. Clean it up. Yeah, just like that. Can you get it open?"

Carter stuck the blade of his shovel under the edge and pried. "Yeah, I think so. It should come open."

"Get the fuck out of there. Guys, drag him up." Hands were all over him, pulling at him, lifting him, and in seconds, he was lying on the dirt at the edge of the hole while Angelico stared down into the hole.

"Got a light?" one of them called up.

"You got a light in that fuckin' truck?" Angelico barked.

"Yeah. Under the front seat. Long silver flashlight."

"Go get it, dumbass." They watched as the guy ambled over to the truck, found the light, and brought it back. "Now we get to see what we've been looking for all these years." Angelico trained the light down into the hole and Carter leaned over just enough to see what was there.

Bags. Canvas bags. He had to believe they were full

of money. And there, sitting on a huge Harley Davidson Electra Glide, was a skeleton, its bony hands gripping the bars and its head lying about three feet away. "Lost your head there, Don Eduardo!" Angelico cackled, and the other guys laughed too. Carter could see with no trouble that the ring finger of the corpse was missing. The rumors were true. That big, tacky ring on Angelico's hand had indeed come from that corpse, and it appeared Taliq had quite a sense of humor to boot. "Get down in there, Weasel, and check out those bags." One of the men jumped down into the metal enclosure and threw a bag out. When Angelico picked it up, money fell out onto the ground. "Aha! There it is! After all these years." He kissed a stack of what looked like twenties, then turned to Carter. "Looks like you've outlived your usefulness. Boys, get that money out of there and put the cop down there. Nobody will ever find him. Hell, look how long it took us to find it! But I'll send you to your grave with one thought. I'll keep my word. Your woman and those kids are safe. We don't need them for anything. The cops already know us, so it's not like they're going to spill any beans, and we have no use for them. But it's time to go, so get your ass on down there in that hole and stay put. Here. Take a bottle of water. You'll survive an extra day with that." Angelico threw the bottle down into the top of the enclosure and pointed for Carter to follow it.

This is it, Carter thought as he walked toward the gaping maw of the excavation. That was when he caught it, something he recognized immediately. Through all the odors of rust, oil, rotting tires, and old gasoline, rolled the slight but distinctive smell of something only a law enforcement officer would recognize—brand-new Kevlar. Carter did the only thing he could think to do.

He sat down.

"What the fuck are you doing?" Angelico screamed.

"I'm sitting right here. You'll have to drag me down there or shoot me."

"Not a problem. Boys, get up here and throw the pig into the pig sty." The two men who'd dropped down into the hole scrambled up as the others stood with their weapons. They were all above ground and that was exactly what Carter wanted.

Something whizzed through the air and he squeezed his eyes shut just before the flash bang cannister went off. There was a lot of smoke, and yelling, and gunfire. He was scrambling, crawling, clawing, trying to get out of the middle of that infernal hell when he felt something on his neck. There was more yelling and gunfire, and he rolled toward a stack of crushed cars out of the middle of the melee. As soon as he was tucked away under the edge of something rusted and red, he slapped his hand on his neck, and when he drew it away, it was drenched.

Blood. Too much blood. Carter pressed against his neck, and he could feel it oozing between his fingers. *Shit. I've got to find somebody or make somebody see me.* He tried to roll, but it was too hard. The gunfire was quieting, and he wondered if anyone could hear him if he called out. "Guys! Hey, guys! Over here!" was all he could think to yell.

He could hear a distinctive Texas drawl in the voice wafting out over the carnage. "Carter? Carter! You out there? CARTER! It's Cruz, Carter! Where are you? He's not down there."

"Where the hell is he?" another voice asked.

"Hey!" His voice was thin and small to his own ears, and a buzzing sound had set up in his head. "Guys! Over here!" He felt weak, too weak to move. Couldn't they hear him? Or see him?

A sudden beam of light pierced the darkness and he heard a voice yell, "There! He's over there!" Footsteps came closer and he looked up. "Carter! He's over here! Hey, buddy. It's okay. We're gonna get you out of here," the voice said, and he caught enough of a glimpse to see a headful of blond hair. Sam.

"I'm … Look," he said, turning his hand over.

"I NEED AN EMT OVER HERE STAT!" he heard Sam scream, but Carter couldn't speak. He wanted to ask if he was going to be okay, if there was as much blood as he thought, but he couldn't. All he could do was lie there in the dirt and a pool of his own blood and think about Sharla.

If only …

CHAPTER 10

Light pierced the darkness and Carter looked around. The blood was gone from his hand, and he sat up, banging his head on the crushed car above him. "Owww!" he muttered, rubbing the spot.

"Come on. Let me help you up," a familiar voice said, and the hand that took his seemed made for it. When Carter looked up, it was into eyes he'd known since childhood.

"Dad! You're here!" He couldn't believe what he was seeing. But where were all the other officers? "What's going on? How did you get here?"

"We need to talk, son. I've been watching you. All you do is say, 'if only, if only, if only.' Carter Mason Melton, you can't live your life that way."

"That's right, son," another voice spoke, and he turned to find Grandpa Ronald standing there, Grandma Frances standing right behind him. "Your daddy knows what he's talking about. Go back, Carter. Stop telling yourself 'if only.' All you have is today. Make it count."

"But I want to stay here with you! Please? I don't want to go back!"

His dad smiled. "What about Sharla and those two kids, Carter? They need you. We don't. Go back, son, and stop looking behind you. Look forward ... look forward ... look forward ..."

"BP's eighty over fifty. We've got the bleeding stopped for now. ETA five minutes."

"Roger that, Mercy three. Standing by."

"Sheriff Melton? Sheriff Melton, can you hear me?"

Carter couldn't figure out what was going on. "Ummmm ..."

"Sheriff Melton, you're in an ambulance heading to O'Fallon General. We'll be there in just a few minutes." A pair of kind eyes looked down into his. "We've got the bleeding stopped. I don't know if you'll need surgery or not, but you're safe for now."

"Uhhhh ..." Carter managed before everything went dark.

When he saw light again, it was a giant, round thing. "We're going to have to do some repairs. Get a surgical suite set up. Ten minutes to prep. Let's go, people," a voice said right beside him. He wanted to ask questions, wanted to know if Sharla was okay, but he was too weak to talk. There was a sensation that he knew was the release of the brakes on his gurney, and they wheeled him toward what he assumed was the operating room. But as they ran along, another face joined them.

"Carter, I'm here. We're all here. Sharla's fine. The

kids are fine. You're gonna be fine. We'll all be waiting for you, buddy. It's going to be okay." That deep, Texas swagger washed over him and he knew Cruz would take care of everything.

They were okay. Sharla and the kids were out of danger. He didn't know what would happen to him, but it didn't matter as long as they were all right.

HE COULD FEEL SOMEONE JOSTLING HIS LEG. IT WAS okay—it wasn't like it hurt—but it was annoying as hell. "Cut it out," he mumbled.

"Hey! He's coming around! Get a nurse! Carter? Hey, bud, it's Cruz. Open your eyes." Carter tried, but he couldn't. "Come on. You're a tough old dog. You can do it." As soon as they fluttered open, Cruz smiled. "Welcome back to the world of the living!"

"Sharla ..."

"Sam's gone to get her. She'll be here in just a second. She was walking your mom down to the car."

"How ..." He couldn't get the words out. Then another face appeared.

"Hi, sir! How ya feelin'?"

Carter was confused. "Edwards?"

"Yes, sir. Everything's under control at the office, sir. Lewis and Durst are taking care of everything."

Carter looked from man to man just as Sam stepped into the room. The blond officer grinned at Carter and asked, "What?"

"How on earth did you find me?"

Cruz laughed. "We'll let Edwards field that question. Deputy?"

"Sir, I lied." Carter couldn't understand. "You're not the only one who can memorize numbers, sir. I can too. Pretty easily, in fact. Been doing it all my life."

Carter didn't get to say another word before he heard a voice shriek, "Carter!" In seconds, Sharla was on him, kissing his forehead, his cheeks, his eyelids, his lips, his chin. "Oh, my god, you're awake!"

"Yeah, yeah."

Then he heard her sniffle and realized her face was coated with tears. "We thought we'd lost you, babe. Oh, god, don't do something stupid like that again, please?"

"I'd only do something that stupid for you," he assured her.

He got a stern glare back from that. "Why doesn't that make me feel a bit better?"

"Weeeeee'll just be out here, trying not to listen and laugh," Sam announced, but it was too late. Cruz and Edwards were already laughing.

"Boy, is he in trou-ble," Edwards was saying as they left.

"Sharla," he started, then stopped.

"What, baby?"

"Sharla, I … I …"

"What is it, Carter?"

"I saw my dad, Sharla. My dad and my grandparents."

Her face went pale. "Oh, god. No."

"Yeah. They were there, in the scrap yard. And they told me to come back, and to not always be thinking 'if only' anymore. They told me to come back for you." He couldn't hold it back anymore—a lone tear trickled out the outer corner of one eye and down his cheek. "Sharla, I'm so sorry. I'm sorry I didn't spend time with you, I'm sorry I did this and almost wasn't here for you, I'm sorry I couldn't keep you safe like I promised, keep the kids safe like I promised, I'm sorry ..."

"Shut up, Carter."

"Huh?"

Sharla smiled down at him. "What did your dad and your grandparents tell you?"

He sighed. "No more 'if only'."

"Yeah. And you're doing it again. This is over. It's a new day. But I can tell you this." She leaned down until her nose was almost touching his. "If you ever do something like this again, go off rogue by yourself, you won't have to worry about the bad guys. When I catch up to you, I'll kill you myself. Understand?" Then she kissed his forehead.

"Roger that." He smiled up at her and wondered if he asked her to marry him, would she say yes.

But he'd wait until he could kneel for that one.

"HERE YA GO." A DRINK, SOMETHING FRUITY WITH AN umbrella in it, appeared in front of his face.

"Seriously? A girly drink?"

Sharla laughed and shaded her eyes with her hand. "It's got bourbon in it."

"Ah, that's more like it!" Carter took a sip first. Not bad. Then he took a bigger swallow.

Yanking the towel from the chaise lounge beside him, Sharla sat down and leaned back. "How are you feeling?"

"I'm good. They get off okay this morning?"

"Yeah. They were so excited." Chelsea and Lionel had never gotten a chance to go to the big theme park when they were growing up, so Carter's first act as their prospective stepdad was to make arrangements to take them. They'd argued with Sharla that she and Carter should come, but she told them to go on. Carter needed to rest and get back to his old self, and the two young people were more than old enough to entertain themselves in the theme park. "I hate to ask, but have you given that offer some thought?"

"I have." As soon as he'd become stable, he'd gotten a visit from Jesse Talbert and Jesse's boss, Harmon Peterson, with an offer of a position at KDCI. Carter had been surprised and flattered, and he really had been thinking about it. "And I know my answer."

He made her wait until she finally cried out, "Oh, for god's sake, Carter, what is it?"

"No."

"No? But why? This would be great for you—for us! More money, better position—"

"You mean *safer* position, right?" Carter said and turned to stare into her eyes.

"Yeah, okay, safer position. Why wouldn't you take it?"

He sat up, dropped his legs off the side of the lounge, and faced her. "Have you ever done something and known it was the exact right thing? Or been somewhere and known you were exactly where you were supposed to be at exactly the right time?"

He could see her deflate a little when she answered, "Yeah. I have."

"That's how I feel about being sheriff of Trigg County. Yeah, that KDCI position would be a safer position, and more money. But the people of my county, they need me. They wouldn't have elected me sheriff if they didn't. And I love them, babe. Yeah, you guys are my family, but so are they. Those guys in my department? They're my brothers. If I don't get re-elected, then yeah—maybe it's time for me to go. But right now, no. I can't. Matter of fact, I don't want to. I hope you're okay with that."

"I guess I'm moving to Trigg County, right?" she asked and winked.

"I guess you are." She had no idea he'd been looking at a bigger house and had already bought a ring. That was on a need-to-know basis and right that minute, she didn't need to know. They were in Kentucky, so it didn't matter how old her daughter and her nephew were. He could still adopt them, and if being his children was what they wanted, he had every intention of doing just that.

Carter Melton loved his job. He loved Sharla, he

DEANNDRA HALL

loved the kids she brought to him, and he loved the guys he worked with. He loved his mom too.

And he loved the food at the resort, but some of Wilda Fern's chicken 'n dumplins sure would've been good right that minute.

ABOUT THE AUTHOR ...

Deanndra Hall is a working author living in the far western end of the beautiful Bluegrass State with her husband of over 35 years and small menagerie of weird little dogs. When she's not writing, she's editing. When she's doing neither of those two things, she's having dinner with friends, spending time with family, kayaking, eating chocolate, drinking beer or moonshine, or looking for something that she put in the wrong place and can't seem to find (which is pretty much everything she owns).

On the Web: www.deanndrahall.com
Email: Deanndra@deanndrahall.com
Facebook: facebook.com/deanndra.hall
Twitter: twitter.com/DeanndraHall
Goodreads: goodreads.com/DeanndraHall
Bookbub: bookbub.com/authors/deanndra-hall

Stay in touch. For all the latest news, contests, exclusive content and more sign up for my newsletter: www.subscribepage.com/deanndrahall

There are many more books in this fan fiction world than listed here, for an up-to-date list go to www.AcesPress.com

You can also visit our Amazon page at:
http://www.amazon.com/author/operationalpha

Special Forces: Operation Alpha World
Denise Agnew: Dangerous to Hold
Shauna Allen: Awakening Aubrey
Shauna Allen: Defending Danielle
Shauna Allen: Rescuing Rebekah
Shauna Allen: Saving Scarlett
Shauna Allen: Saving Grace
Brynne Asher: Blackburn
Jennifer Becker: Hiding Catherine
Julia Bright: Saving Lorelei
Julia Bright: Rescuing Amy
Victoria Bright: Surviving Savage
Victoria Bright: Going Ghost
Victoria Bright: Jostling Joker
Cara Carnes: Protecting Mari
Kendra Mei Chailyn: Beast
Kendra Mei Chailyn: Barbie
Kendra Mei Chailyn : Pitbull
Melissa Kay Clarke: Rescuing Annabeth
Melissa Kay Clarke: Safeguarding Miley
Samantha A. Cole: Handling Haven
Samantha A. Cole: Cheating the Devil
Sue Coletta: Hacked

Melissa Combs: Gallant
KaLyn Cooper: Rescuing Melina
Liz Crowe: Marking Mariah
Jordan Dane: Redemption for Avery
Jordan Dane: Fiona's Salvation
Riley Edwards: Protecting Olivia
Riley Edwards: Redeeming Violet
Riley Edwards, Recovering Ivy
Nicole Flockton: Protecting Maria
Nicole Flockton: Guarding Erin
Nicole Flockton: Guarding Suzie
Nicole Flockton: Guarding Brielle
Casey Hagen: Shielding Nebraska
Casey Hagen: Shielding Harlow
Casey Hagen: Shielding Josie
Casey Hagen: Shielding Blair
Desiree Holt: Protecting Maddie
Kathy Ivan: Saving Sarah
Kathy Ivan: Saving Savannah
Kathy Ivan: Saving Stephanie
Jesse Jacobson: Protecting Honor
Jesse Jacobson: Fighting for Honor
Jesse Jacobson: Defending Honor
Jesse Jacobson: Summer Breeze
Silver James: Rescue Moon
Silver James: SEAL Moon
Silver James: Assassin's Moon
Silver James: Under the Assassin's Moon
Becca Jameson: Saving Sofia
Kate Kinsley: Protecting Ava

Heather Long: Securing Arizona

Heather Long: Guarding Gertrude

Heather Long: Protecting Pilar

Heather Long: Covering Coco

Gennita Low: No Protection

Kirsten Lynn: Joining Forces for Jesse

Margaret Madigan: Bang for the Buck

Margaret Madigan: Buck the System

Margaret Madigan: Jungle Buck

Margaret Madigan: December Chill

Rachel McNeely: The SEAL's Surprise Baby

Rachel McNeely: The SEAL's Surprise Bride

Rachel McNeely: The SEAL's Surprise Twin

KD Michaels: Saving Laura

KD Michaels: Protecting Shane

KD Michaels: Avenging Angels

Wren Michaels: The Fox & The Hound

Wren Michaels: The Fox & The Hound 2

Wren Michaels: Shadow of Doubt

Wren Michaels: Shift of Fate

Wren Michaels: Steeling His Heart

Kat Mizera: Protecting Bobbi

Mary B Moore: Force Protection

LeTeisha Newton: Protecting Butterfly

LeTeisha Newton: Protecting Goddess

LeTeisha Newton: Protecting Vixen

LeTeisha Newton: Protecting Heartbeat

MJ Nightingale: Protecting Beauty

MJ Nightingale: Betting on Benny

MJ Nightingale: Protecting Secrets

Sarah O'Rourke: Saving Liberty
Debra Parmley: Protecting Pippa
Lainey Reese: Protecting New York
Jenika Snow: Protecting Lily
Jen Talty: Burning Desire
Jen Talty: Burning Kiss
Jen Talty: Burning Skies
Jen Talty: Burning Lies
Jen Talty: Burning Heart
Megan Vernon: Protecting Us
Megan Vernon: Protecting Earth

Fire and Police: Operation Alpha World

Freya Barker: Burning for Autumn
KaLyn Cooper: Justice for Gwen
Aspen Drake: Sheltering Emma
Barb Han: Kace
Reina Torres: Justice for Sloane
Stacey Wilk: Stage Fright

As you know, this book included at least one character from Susan Stoker's books. To check out more, see below.

SEAL of Protection: Legacy Series

Securing Caite
Securing Brenae (novella)
Securing Sidney (May 2019)
Securing Piper (Aug 2019)
Securing Zoey (Jan 2020)
Securing Avery (TBA)
Securing Kalee (TBA)

Delta Force Heroes Series

Rescuing Rayne (FREE!)
Rescuing Aimee
Rescuing Emily
Rescuing Harley
Marrying Emily
Rescuing Kassie
Rescuing Bryn
Rescuing Casey
Rescuing Sadie
Rescuing Wendy
Rescuing Mary
Rescuing Macie

Badge of Honor: Texas Heroes Series

Justice for Mackenzie (FREE!)
Justice for Mickie

Justice for Corrie
Justice for Laine (novella)
Shelter for Elizabeth
Justice for Boone
Shelter for Adeline
Shelter for Sophie
Justice for Erin
Justice for Milena
Shelter for Blythe
Justice for Hope
Shelter for Quinn
Shelter for Koren (July 2019)
Shelter for Penelope (Oct 2019)

SEAL of Protection Series
Protecting Caroline (FREE!)
Protecting Alabama
Protecting Fiona
Marrying Caroline (novella)
Protecting Summer
Protecting Cheyenne
Protecting Jessyka
Protecting Julie (novella)
Protecting Melody
Protecting the Future
Protecting Kiera (novella)
Protecting Alabama's Kids (novella)
Protecting Dakota

New York Times, USA Today and *Wall Street Journal*

Bestselling Author Susan Stoker has a heart as big as the state of Tennessee where she lives, but this all American girl has also spent the last fourteen years living in Missouri, California, Colorado, Indiana, and Texas. She's married to a retired Army man who now gets to follow *her* around the country.

She debuted her first series in 2014 and quickly followed that up with the SEAL of Protection Series, which solidified her love of writing and creating stories readers can get lost in.

If you enjoyed this book, or any book, please consider leaving a review. It's appreciated by authors more than you'll know.

www.stokeraces.com
www.AcesPress.com
susan@stokeraces.com

Made in United States
Cleveland, OH
18 March 2025

15284440R00148